WAIT FOR YOU

FIREWEED HARBOR SERIES

J.H. CROIX

 Created with Vellum

To every woman who found her way through.

Sign up for my newsletter for information on new releases & get a FREE copy of one of my books!

http://jhcroixauthor.com/subscribe/

Follow me!
jhcroix@jhcroix.com
https://amazon.com/author/jhcroix
https://www.bookbub.com/authors/j-h-croix
https://www.facebook.com/jhcroix
https://www.instagram.com/jhcroix/

Chapter One

TESSA

Me: *Do you happen to have Adam's number?*

Five minutes pass, and I fervently wish I could un-send the text I just sent to my friend.

McKenna: *Adam? My brother Adam?*

I hesitated for a moment, my heart pounding unsteadily in my chest and my belly twisting with churning anxiety. What white lie could I tell one of my closest friends so she would give me her brother's phone number?

Me: *Yeah. I had his phone number in my contacts, but when I got my new phone, I lost some of them.*

Okay, that was actually true, so I wasn't lying.

Me: *I need to ask him an accounting question. He said something about some kind of software he recommended. You know how much I hate doing my taxes.*

I *did* hate doing my taxes, so that was only kind of a lie. And I *had* overheard Adam recommending some tax program to someone at the potluck. So really, it was all true. Of course, spring and tax season had just passed, but that was a minor detail.

Ha! My cynical mind mocked me.

McKenna is too busy being in love to worry about why I need her brother's phone number, I told myself.

A second later, she shared his contact. I bit my lip. With seven siblings, the Cannon family was unusually large in this modern day.

I giggled when I saw what McKenna named this brother in her contacts. *Adam #4. The smart one.*

My heart kicked a little faster again, and my belly still spun from my encounter with Adam hours ago. He'd set off a chain reaction in me. I felt reckless.

After my disaster of a marriage and divorce over a year and a half ago, I hadn't dated. At all. I convinced myself that was fine. It *was* fine. I didn't want a relationship.

I just wanted to see if I could kiss a man and not be terrified. I trusted Adam. Or I thought I did. Trust wasn't a familiar feeling for me. Not with men.

Before I lost my courage and that streak of recklessness was trampled by common sense and the fear that had ruled my life for too many years, I tapped the contact and saved it in my phone. I renamed it simply *Adam*.

Opening up a text window, I typed out a text.

Me: *Maybe this is crazy, but I wanted to take you up on your offer.*

I hit send before I could chicken out and set my phone on the bed. My pulse galloped along so fast I could hardly catch my breath, and all I was doing was sitting in bed alone.

When no reply came for over a minute, a familiar feeling began to rise, a churning sense of panic. It felt like water creeping up my ankles while I was trapped inside a room with nowhere to go. That was how I had felt for... I paused as I mentally calculated.

I was still in college when I started dating Rich. He asked me to marry him six months into our relationship, and I said yes. The next day, he hit me for the first time. That was after months of verbal put-downs and jabs. I should've backed out. But I was ashamed, and I believed him when he apologized. I thought it would never happen again. I thought it would get better.

My life then played out like a textbook on emotional, verbal, and physical abuse. I felt completely alone, like no one could ever have been as stupid as I was. Before I knew it, we were married. I rode the whiplash of days of quiet, punctuated by verbal jabs and insults, occasional hits to objects and me. Then he'd calm down. Around and around and around we went. When I was pregnant, he threatened to kill me. I stayed until I learned to cry in complete and utter silence in the darkness and didn't know if I could ever get out. By that point, it felt as if the water had risen to my chin and occasionally a little higher, and I feared I would drown.

But my son or, as my ex insisted on emphasizing, *our* son made me want to fight. One day, something just broke inside me. I left with nothing more than a backpack of my clothes, my son, and two bags for him.

As I sat there by myself, I fidgeted, wondering what had set off my panic. While I cataloged the anxiety zipping through me, I realized waiting for a text response was a trauma trigger for me. Because Rich used to do that to me all the time. I couldn't ever re-call him replying to a text quickly. I always had to wait.

Doubts clamored loudly in my brain, shouting that Adam couldn't have meant what he said. That I wasn't cute, that he didn't want to kiss me, that I was absolutely out of my freaking mind to have sent him this text.

Just as I lifted my phone to type in a follow-up message, it vibrated with a response. I swallowed through the tightness in my throat and stared at Adam's response.

Adam: *The offer to kiss you?*

Fiery heat flashed into my cheeks. "Oh my God, oh my God, oh my God," I said out loud.

My pulse went wild, and a warm, tingly sensation built in my belly.

Adam: *Any time. Just say when and where.*

Oh my God, oh my God, oh my God, oh my God!

"Mom!"

"Oh fuck!" I whispered quickly before kicking back the covers on my bed and scrambling to my bedroom door. "Yeah?"

"Why are you saying 'oh my God' over and over?" Eric asked.

"Oh my fucking God," I whispered under

my breath. Six-year-olds could be so nosy and had really good hearing.

"I stubbed my toe. I promise I'm fine."

For good measure, I opened the door. My son's worried face was right there, his brown hair sticking straight up. He wore pajamas with bears all over them and had the cutest little toes. These were the silly details mothers noticed all the time.

I hated the look of worry on his face, and I hated even more that I understood where it came from. He had heard many arguments through closed doors and walls when we still lived with his father. As a result, he was hypervigilant. According to his therapist and my therapist and the women I'd met in a support group I went to after I somehow escaped the hellhole of my marriage, this was an expected response. He was constantly attuned to every little reaction from the adults in his world.

Eric blinked, and I watched as the tension softened in his face. "Okay."

"Why are you still awake?" I asked as I leaned my shoulder inside the doorframe.

"I was reading my comics." He held up his comic book.

"Okay, lights out in..." I glanced at my

watch. "A half an hour ago." I gave him a pointed look, and he grinned.

"Okay, I'll go to sleep now."

I watched as he trotted across the hallway to his bedroom at an angle across from mine. I waited until he closed the door and the light disappeared from under the doorway a moment later.

I took a deep breath. Just recently, Eric told me he didn't want me to tuck him in every night. Every time I thought about that, I experienced a pang in my heart. He was growing up so fast. In some ways, he was so old for his years.

I padded into the kitchen and got a glass of ice water. After a few sips, I returned to my bedroom and looked down at the phone. All of my recklessness had dissipated. I just felt like a frumpy, un-sexy mom.

I debated not even replying to Adam. I could try to play it off and tell him I had texted the wrong number. But when I reached for my phone, another text from him awaited me.

Adam: *I'm guessing you're freaking out. No need. I'd still like to kiss you, but please don't stress over it. Good night, Tessa.*

I swallowed as my heart began racing

again. I was hot all over. It's not that I'd never noticed Adam Cannon before. He was handsome, like all of his brothers. But I had trained myself to never pay attention to any other man during my marriage. Never. It wasn't safe.

Just remembering that brought a surge of courage and adrenaline flooding through me. Lifting my phone, I replied.

Me: *I'd like that kiss. Promise?*

Chapter Two

ADAM

Tessa's last text played on a loop. *I'd like that kiss. Promise?*

It was a little echo in my thoughts. I imagined hearing it in her low, raspy voice.

I didn't know what happened the other night when I encountered her in the hallway at my sister's dinner party, but it felt like a door had been kicked open inside me. Awareness and need rushed through, the force of it intense enough that I couldn't ignore it.

Tessa was beyond cute and sexy as hell. I was still marveling that I hadn't noticed her like that before. I knew what McKenna would say if she knew my thoughts. For starters, my only sister had pointed out many times that I was closed off ever since Julie died.

As if I didn't have enough baggage in my life growing up. Our family had plenty of messy dynamics, with our father dying and our abusive grandfather running through our family like a wrecking ball. I craved stability in my life when I was in high school. Julie had given me that. She'd been pretty and nice, and we fell in love.

She died during our freshman year in college in a cycling accident. Even worse, I found out after she died that she'd been planning to break up with me. College had been a new social world for us. While I'd craved stability and familiarity, she'd wanted something else. I would never know all the details, but she'd started chatting with some guy. I wasn't mad at her, not even then, but it hurt. I knew what I felt for her had been young and childish and that nobody could've ever lived up to my expectations, but I still carried a touch of bitterness.

I didn't know what the hell happened the other night, but that moment with Tessa had been like dry grass catching fire inside.

I'd answered Tessa's text with, *Promise*.

The question remained as to when I would keep my promise to her.

I was impatient to see her, champing at the bit. For the first time, I found myself looking around town, constantly wondering when I might see her in passing. Fireweed Harbor was a small town. For years, I'd been glad to be away from my hometown. Seattle had suited me when we had our corporation's headquarters there. I could be invisible. I didn't have to worry about my family's history hanging over me like a dark cloud.

I was irritated when Rhys insisted on moving the headquarters back to Fireweed Harbor. Surprisingly, it had created a sense of freedom for me. Old wounds healed and all that. As a family, we were doing much better. Yet while my siblings fell like dominoes into love, I hadn't even felt the slightest inclination.

Tessa had never come to mind in this way for me. Yet I couldn't stop thinking about her now. The subtle flush on her skin. Her big brown eyes. The way I could hear the shallow pants of her breath. The way it had taken almost every ounce of my discipline not to kiss her the other night. Just one brief encounter had lit a flame.

I forced myself to focus on my work. I could lose myself in numbers. I enjoyed numbers because understanding them came to me easily. They were orderly and pre-dictable.

I was working late after the office had closed when I heard Tessa's voice. "Okay, I'm just going to stop in the bathroom. Is that okay?"

She must've come to meet my sister McKenna for some reason. Her voice was like a crack of lightning just after thunder rumbled through the sky in my nervous system.

I waited for McKenna's response. "Of course. I have to hurry over to the winery because I told Jack I'd be there already, and I'm late. The doors downstairs lock automat-ically, so don't worry about it. I'll meet you there."

My pulse lunged, and impatience crackled inside me. I waited for McKenna's footsteps to disappear down the hallway. The minutes ticked by until I heard Tessa come out of the bathroom.

"Tessa," I called.

My voice was low, but I hoped it was loud enough for her to hear me. I heard her steps approaching. There was a hesitation in her stride before she stopped in the doorway. She studied me for a moment.

"Adam," she finally said. "You're working late."

My eyes never left hers. I lifted one shoulder in a shrug. "I usually do."

I stood from my desk, then crossed the office and stopped a few feet from her. She stood just inside the door. It felt like a force field began to vibrate between us, the voltage intense and electric.

"Well?" I prompted.

My gruff voice conveyed my frayed control. I didn't have to be specific. I could tell by the look in her eyes that she knew what I was referring to.

Tessa took a step closer. My fingers itched to reach beyond her and close the door. But this had to be her choice entirely.

Her hand curled over the doorknob before she closed it with a decisive click. A flush rose on her cheeks, and my lungs tightened. Every cell in my body fired.

And still, I waited.

She took another step closer until she was immediately in front of me. My thoughts flicked back to the other night when I'd encountered her in the hallway at the dinner party. It was as if a path had formed between us. Heat and electricity shimmered in the space now.

"Tessa?" I prompted when I saw hesitation flicker in her eyes.

I could feel her take a deep breath when her breasts rose against my chest as she took one more incremental step closer. She lifted a palm, placing it in the center of my chest. There was no doubt she could feel the rapid drumbeat of my heart.

"Oh, good," she whispered.

"What's good?"

"Your heart is beating as fast as mine. Maybe." Her lips kicked up at the corner in a wry half-smile.

"Do you still want a kiss?" I asked.

Her swallowing was audible in the near-total silence of my office. All I could hear was the rush of my own heartbeat and the subtle sound of us breathing.

"More than anything." Her voice was a raspy whisper.

I was almost trembling when I lifted a hand and brushed one of her loose curls off her cheek to tuck it behind her ear. Her auburn hair was silky soft. I let my fingers slide into it, lightly cupping the nape of her neck.

My eyes were on her wide brown gaze as I dipped my head. Time felt simultaneously suspended and as if racing forward at a breakneck pace.

Her eyes darkened, her lashes sweeping down just as my lips came within a whisper of hers. I brushed over the plush surface of her lips once and then again. I heard her soft sigh followed by her body melting closer to me.

Finally, fucking *finally*, I angled my head to the side and fit my mouth over hers. Our kiss started slow with a tease of my tongue over the seam of her lips. Our tongues twined together in a lazy tangle when her mouth opened for mine.

I breathed her in, absorbing her scent. The imprint of her soft curves against my body sent electricity sizzling through me. When my fingers tightened in her hair, she let out a sweet little moan in her throat. I took another step, nudging her back until she bumped into the door. I slapped my hand against it, sliding the other over the curve of her shoulder, down along the sweet dip of her waist, and over the generous, lush curve of her hip.

My cock was as hard as a tire iron, burning hot, and nestled in the sweet cradle of her hips. We fit together perfectly. Our kiss went on and on and on, and I felt wild from it by the time we broke apart. My heart pounded in my ears, and my breath came in deep, ragged heaves.

We stared at each other. Her wide eyes were dazed with passion, just as I imagined mine were. I had to claw my way back to thinking, to finding a way to speak.

"You said you wanted a kiss." My voice was guttural. I barely recognized myself.

I couldn't remember the last time I'd felt this out of control. For a second, I thought it had to have been when I was in high school. That was different, though. Youthful, driven by the endless revving of the hormonal engine of adolescence and early adulthood, of the newness of it all.

The cynicism that scored my heart burned through every interaction since then. I'd always felt entirely under control with my hands firmly on the reins. This was beyond all of that. It was the desire cast into streaks of lightning, the winds of the storm blowing it wild and in unexpected directions.

Tessa blinked. "I did ask for a kiss." Her low, throaty voice spun into the heat, nearly burning me up.

I scrambled inside, wanting to feel in control of the situation. Frankly, I wanted to just feel in control of myself. "Is that enough?"

As we stared at each other, it felt as if

something shifted in the air around us and inside me, another door opening.

"No," she said.

As I held her gaze, I thought I saw doubts casting shadows there. She lifted her chin, her tongue sliding across her bottom lip, sending a hot shot of blood to my cock.

"What do you want next?"

Chapter Three

TESSA

I knew from McKenna that Adam was the least likely of her brothers to get serious. I knew his story, even if he and I weren't close. At four years older than McKenna, that was a chasm when we were younger. Adam's girlfriend from high school had died during their freshman year in college. McKenna said he'd been truly devastated. She said he was too cynical to get serious again.

I didn't want a relationship or anything remotely serious. I just wanted a chance to see if I could feel something other than numb. I felt more alive at this moment after a kiss from Adam than I'd maybe ever felt with a man.

Adam's gaze bored into mine. Even

though it was intense, I felt a thread of protectiveness in it. I didn't know if it was conscious on his part. I gathered my courage, daring myself.

"More." That was all I could manage to say.

Adam was quiet for an electrifying moment. Somewhere along the way, his knee had slipped between my thighs, and I could feel the subtle pressure on my clit. It was a sweet, piercing pressure. It was all I could do not to rock my hips.

If I was an expert at one thing, though, it was staying in control and managing every incremental response of my body. I held still until I began to tremble. His hand rested on the curve of my hip. He shifted it slightly, his touch almost soothing. I didn't say a word, but it felt as if he could read my mind.

"It's okay," he said, his tone low.

The tension left my body in a whoosh on the heels of a breath.

"You don't have to do anything. With me, that is," he added.

Quiet fell between us, and I thought for a moment this would be where the conversation ended.

"Tell me what more means."

I marshaled my composure and took a

shaky breath. Tension began to buzz inside. "I don't really..." I took another breath. All the while, he waited patiently. "I don't want a relationship. I've already been married, and it was a disaster."

Adam's nod was almost imperceptible, and I didn't sense any annoyance or impatience from him. I wasn't used to someone waiting to let me explain. It unsettled me, but I forced myself to forge ahead.

"But I don't want to be a nun. And for some reason, I trust you."

His brows hitched up slightly. After a loaded moment of silence, his lips curled at the corners and my belly shimmied. "Well, of course, I don't want to be a priest either. Or we could just say we don't want to be celibate."

I rolled my eyes slightly. I didn't know why I felt so comfortable with Adam. Although he'd been in the periphery of my life when I was growing up, he and I weren't what I would call friends. We were friendly.

"How come you never noticed me before?" I wanted to snatch the question back as soon as it slipped out.

But Adam took it at face value. "I don't know. Maybe because when we were younger, you were my little sister's friend. Because of our family, friends didn't come to our house much. While I knew you were McKenna's friend, you were in the distance, and—" His words cut off abruptly, and he shrugged again.

He didn't need to elaborate on his family. To my knowledge, this generation of the Cannon family was close and loving. Maybe those bonds had been forged in the trauma their grandfather had meted out through abuse.

I didn't even really know the whole story of his experience in his family or how he felt about his girlfriend dying. In short, I knew a lot of details about Adam, but I didn't *know* him beyond a friendly, superficial level.

"How come you never noticed me?" he asked, his gaze curious.

I stared at him, and my heart started to beat faster. I wanted to tell the truth. Before I could say anything, he swore, "Aw, hell, I shouldn't have asked that."

"Why? I asked you," I pointed out.

Silence filled the space again. I was surprised to realize I didn't start panicking. There was a sense of anticipation but not the dread and fear that I used to experience with my ex whenever there were gaps of silence.

"Because I know Rich. He's a controlling,

jealous asshole. I'm guessing you didn't pay attention to anybody because it wasn't safe for you to do that," Adam said, his tone careful and level.

My eyes were wide, and cold fear drafted through me. "How well do you know him? Are you friends?" My voice was on the verge of shaking.

Adam's reaction was swift. "Fuck, no. He was a bully when we were kids, he was an asshole in high school, and he was a fucking asshole in college. I know him because Fireweed Harbor is a small town. Like I mentioned before, he was a controlling, jealous jerk with a girl he dated. He freaked out about some guy holding the door for her in the winter once. I don't have to know him well to get the idea. He has a reputation." Adam studied me for several long beats while my heart pounded against my ribs. "Why do you trust me?"

I contemplated his question, trying to read my body's reaction to him, almost reaching for slivers of doubt. "I don't know."

A tiny corner of my mind was afraid I would be wrong, because I hadn't had a reason to mistrust Rich at first. Yet the way I felt with Adam was nothing like that.

Once again, silence stretched between us. "What does 'more' mean?" he finally asked.

I could barely breathe with the force of anticipation seizing my lungs and sending my pulse skittering. "Just that. More."

Adam nodded, and I suddenly became aware that we'd been having this emotionally fraught conversation, and all the while, his knee was nestled between my thighs. My panties were wet, and my nipples were tight, and I had forgotten all of it.

Just as I flailed about, trying to figure out how to exit this moment gracefully, Adam said, "Just tell me when and where. It's always on your terms."

I knew, to my bones, that he meant that.

Chapter Four

ADAM

It's always on your terms.

My own words played through my thoughts on repeat. I'd meant what I'd said. Yet it was turning out to be more difficult than I could've imagined. I fucking *wanted* Tessa. And now, I was waiting. For her.

I was practical enough to be aware of what it meant for her to be a single mom. Maybe I didn't know much about her life, but I suspected she was busy. Inconveniently, when I was stopping by the grocery store, the very evening after I saw her in the office, I saw her ex Rich in the grocery store. He was on the phone. He was one of the guys who talked on the phone as though he wasn't in the middle of everywhere, just oblivious to anything going on around him. He'd been in line, and the young guy at the register had to wait while Rich bitched to someone about preferring to cancel his visit with his son, but knowing it wouldn't look good with the court.

I wanted to clock the guy. Well, not really. I'd never laid a hand on anyone.

The following afternoon, I was deep into analyzing a budgetary plan for an expansion when my twin brother Kenan knocked on my door before peering inside.

"Hey, hey."

I smiled out of habit and because I was almost always glad to see Kenan. We were so different, yet we knew each other so well.

"What's up?" He strolled into my office, plunking in the chair directly across from my desk. He immediately reached for a Slinky that I kept there solely for him. Kenan was one of those fidgety people who always did something with his hands.

"Just looking at our plans for expanding the operations in Willow Brook and adding a new location down in Seattle," I explained.

"For offices?" His brow furrowed in confusion.

"Oh no. We're done with offices there. Another distribution location for the renewable batteries we're producing in Willow Brook."

Kenan nodded. "Ah, I knew this." He flashed a grin.

"You always know everything," I returned with a brow waggle.

"Well, not everything, and I definitely never know when you or Rhys might change your mind."

I rolled my eyes and glanced down to tap Save on my computer.

My brother sobered after a beat. "Have you seen Mom lately?"

"I see her every week," I said. We all did. We were close. All of us.

"Quinn mentioned she stopped by to drop something off and said Mom seems down, I guess, ever since McKenna finally talked about things."

I held my brother's gaze. "I know," I finally said, an old, achy pain sharpening in my heart.

As one of eight siblings whose oldest brother drank himself to death before graduating from college, it was fair to say our family history was a tangled mess.

"Do you think there's more she doesn't know?" Kenan asked, his eyes worried.

I took a slow breath. Kenan and I were

smack in the middle of the family. We had two older brothers, a younger set of twin brothers, and a younger sister. We probably knew the most about everyone in the family from our vantage point.

The one secret none of us had known, except for our cousin Archer, had been that Jake had been sexually abused by our grandfather. The same grandfather who had been verbally abusive to all of us and physically abusive to Jake, Rhys, and Blake.

Kenan and I knew most of the rest, but only bits and pieces. Jake had had a terrible temper, and our sister, McKenna, had been the target of his bullying. While we'd never spoken of it when we were kids, we tried to protect her when we could.

Somehow, I felt like the one who had to carry all of it.

I shrugged because I didn't know the answer. "I'm just glad McKenna finally talked to Mom."

"And Wyatt?" Kenan prompted.

Griffin and Wyatt were the other twins and had only recently moved back to Fireweed Harbor. Wyatt never said why, but you could sometimes feel his distance.

"That's his story."

Siblings were messy sometimes. We all kept each other's secrets.

We were the peacekeepers. Kenan was the one who did everything anybody needed to keep the peace and the joker who tried to lighten every tense moment. I was the more serious one, the one who dared Jake to hit me instead of McKenna. Jake never took me up on that.

"Mom will be okay. We'll all be okay," I added.

Kenan tended to be more serious with me than with the larger group of us. I would never know, but sometimes it felt like we'd made a deal before we were ever born. We would take care of each other and the rest of the family.

Kenan drummed his fingertips on the arm of the chair before he nodded once sharply.

"How's blissful married life?" I wanted to shift gears in this conversation.

Kenan had finally come to his senses and married his best friend, Quinn.

A wide smile cracked across his face. "It's blissful."

I chuckled. "You're set for life."

Kenan murmured a sound of agreement before angling his head to the side and studying me. "What about you?" My twin was more perceptive than he let on. He always had been.

"What do you mean?" I hedged.

"Are you set for life?"

I shrugged lightly. "Maybe."

With anyone other than my twin, I might've flatly insisted I was. But Kenan knew better. He was the only person I'd ever told about discovering Julie had wanted to break up. It wasn't that I thought we would've been together forever. It burned that she hadn't talked to me about it.

For a split second, I wanted to ask him what he knew about Tessa. I knew Tessa, but she'd always been on the edges of my life. Quinn was one of her closest friends, so I had no doubt Kenan encountered her often since he'd gotten married.

"What is it?" he prompted.

Kenan wasn't an actual mind reader. He didn't know I wanted to ask about Tessa. He just knew I wanted to ask about something.

"Nothing."

A sly gleam entered his gaze. "You'll ask me at some point, so you might as well cut to the chase."

A dry laugh rustled in my throat. "True enough. When the time is right."

"Fine." He stood from his chair, tapping

his knuckles on my desk. "For what it's worth, I don't think you're cut out to be alone for the rest of your life."

This wasn't the first time he'd made that observation. Until that brief encounter with Tessa, I would've dismissed it. Now, I was busy trying to tell myself I could keep the boundaries in my heart delineated.

After Kenan left my office, my eyes slid to my cell phone where it sat silently on my desk. I wasn't a guy who waited for texts. Yet with Tessa, I was. I had lobbed the ball into her court, and now I waited.

Chapter Five

TESSA

Rich kept his eyes pinned on me. I resisted the urge to curl my arms around my waist to shield myself.

"Hurry up," he barked at Eric.

Rich didn't even look at Eric. This was how it went when I dropped my son off for visits with his father. Rich had visits every other weekend, and he often cut them short. I resisted the urge to ask what his plans were.

If I said a word about it, he would change his plans. The man was mercurial about everything. If he knew I expected him to give up any time with our son, he wouldn't do it. I remained still and quiet, willing away the urge to nervously chew the insides of my cheeks. Because he would notice that too.

Eric scrambled out of the car. I knew he was reluctant to go with his dad. He always was, yet I couldn't do anything about it. We were still locked in a custody battle. Rich was fighting for fifty percent when he couldn't even be bothered to do an entire weekend.

Rich finally looked away from me when he heard the door to his car close. I waited. "I'm gonna have to cut the weekend short. Just tonight. If you could pick him up tomorrow at my place at two, that would be great," he said.

"I'll meet you here at two." I tried to keep my tone level.

"Fuck this stupid drop-off location. Just come to the fucking house. You used to live there," Rich muttered.

I'd recited responses to him to keep myself from spiraling inside. "You know this is the court-ordered drop-off location. This is where we're meeting."

"Well, then I won't drop him off early." My ex's tone was laced with a hint of "fuck you."

Every time he played these games with me, I knew I had to keep my cool. "It's your weekend, so it's up to you. Please text me if you'd like to meet me here at two tomorrow."

My level, flat tone belied the spinning

anxiety, the dread, and the constant sickening anticipation rising inside me.

"Oh, for fuck's sake. I'll drop him off at two tomorrow. Don't be late."

Rich spun on his heel, stalking away. I stood right where I was, waiting until he'd climbed into his car before I turned and took the three steps to mine. Only after I had closed and locked my car doors did I let out the breath I'd been holding.

Still, I waited, not even looking in the direction of Rich's car. His tires squealed as he left the parking lot. Only after his car was out of sight did I feel the hot tears roll down my cheeks.

I only let myself cry for a minute. Maybe it didn't make sense, but if I let the pain take over, I feared it would drown me. "We got out," I said to myself in the car.

I glanced at the clock on my dashboard before reaching for my phone and typing out a quick text to Eric. I managed so many details of my life as a result of the years with my ex.

The part that hurt the worst, that I hated the most, was that our son carried the same habits as I did. I had told him that he didn't have to do these things, but he said it was easier for all of us. When I was with Rich, I'd always kept my phone notifications turned off. Eric did the same. That way, if his dad demanded to check his phone, he wouldn't have to look for too long. You'd think it wouldn't bother Eric's father for me to text Eric to tell him I loved him. But that's not ever how it went with Rich.

I typed out the text and pasted it into the app Eric and I used to communicate. I read all about how parents should be careful having their kids use chat apps because they could take advantage of each other. I understood those concerns. In my case, I didn't want the message to last long. I wanted Eric to see it and have it disappear in case his father ever paid enough attention to notice the app. I hated that this was what we did. However, my attorney said it was fine, and Eric's therapist also said it was okay.

The days of my clamoring doubts about how it would be worse if I left my ex were long gone. I just hated that he still had a hold over our son and me, by extension.

I love you. Don't forget to look at the stars tonight.

We always looked at the stars together even when things were at their worst.

After putting my phone back into my purse, I pointed my car toward my attorney's office. After that came work. I had a new job, and I loved it. I was a local weather reporter. I'd changed jobs after finally getting away from Rich.

It was so much fun. When I first switched from being a teacher to a weather reporter, the elementary school where I used to work had invited me over for job day to talk about my work. My prior students had asked if they could send in messages for me. It had turned into this game where I would share requests and provide weather information. So far, we'd covered topics like different types of clouds and why volcanic ash could cause car engines to break down.

My program executive had given tentative approval at first, and it had become wildly popular with the station, getting messages from all over Alaska and lots of attention on social media. Kids and parents loved it. I had to ignore the snide comments that my ex made on occasion. He despised anything fun or positive for me.

A few minutes later, I slowed and turned into the parking lot at Blackthorn Partners. I hurried in, waving when Quinn waved at me from her office. She was one of my closest friends. She'd recently admitted she was in love with Kenan Cannon, Adam's twin brother. I said "admitted" because they'd been best friends for years. We'd all thought they belonged together, and they finally got their heads out of their asses and realized it themselves.

With all of these connections to Adam, you'd think I somehow would've been closer to him. But he was the quiet one and kept to himself. As he'd astutely pointed out, my ex was also the jealous type, so I had gone out of my way to never get friendly with any men, even men who were happily married to my friends. It was ridiculous.

I knocked lightly on Colin Blackthorn's open office door. He looked up from his desk and smiled, waving me in. "Come on in, Tessa."

He nudged his chin toward the door when I stepped in without closing it. "Close the door."

My stomach tightened as soon as he said that, and fear began to coil like a snake ready to strike inside. I swallowed. I stopped in front of his desk, resting my fingertips lightly on the edge of it.

"Have a seat." He gestured to the chair behind me.

I clenched a hand tightly onto my purse strap as I sat down. "What is it?" I asked.

"What? No friendly conversation?" Colin's tone was light, but his smile wasn't reaching his eyes now.

I shook my head. "Just get to the point."

"Rich's attorney has filed an amendment. He's no longer filing for full custody."

My eyes widened, but I didn't trust any of this. "Is that good or bad?"

Colin considered me. "Well, Rich has proposed attending co-parenting coaching classes with you."

"No, no, no. Colin, I just dropped Eric off for his weekend visit, and Rich wants me to pick him up tomorrow at two. He doesn't even spend whole weekends with Eric. I just want this over. He doesn't want to do co-parenting classes. He's just trying to find a way to make me miserable." Tears were stinging in my eyes, but I refused to give into them.

I took a slow breath, and Colin slid his handy box of tissues from the corner of the desk closer to me. A bitter laugh slipped out, and I dabbed at my eyes. "You should've bought stock in tissue when you took my case."

"I agree with everything you're saying," Colin said. "I just wanted you to be aware of the filing. We're holding firm on our request for full custody, and I have a bit of good news."

"What's that?"

"The judge on this case is retiring. It's been assigned at our request to a judge in Juneau. While we don't have a choice in judges, I feel good about this one. He—"

"I think it would be better if we got a female judge. I just feel like—"

Colin held a hand up. "I know you feel like a female would understand better. This has been an awful experience because this judge does know Rich's family. He should've recused himself from the case, but we can't change that. He's retiring, so it's no longer relevant. As I explained before, we can't choose the judge. In this case, Rich is less likely to badger a male judge, so I'm good with it. It just is what it is."

This was a fact, so I wouldn't argue that point. Rich had been a nightmare during one hearing covered by a female judge when the primary judge on the case was out of town.

"I'm familiar with the judge in Juneau. He's fair, and he takes no bullshit. There's no way he will force you to do co-parenting classes with Rich."

"Is there any way I can just get this to end?"

Colin studied me quietly. "Unless Rich is willing to relinquish his rights, in which case you'd forgo all child support for the rest of Eric's life."

"I don't want the money. Honestly, I'd rather be homeless and living on a friend's couch if I have to. He doesn't give me much anyway."

I let out a sigh. This wasn't the first time Colin had pointed this out, and I was still reluctant. Even though I knew Rich would never change, there was a thin thread of possibility that he could be a good father. Lately, though, I have felt like our son was truly nothing more than a bargaining chip to his father.

"It's not something you can do anyway. It's just the only way to stop all this time in court."

"It's been almost two years." My voice sounded as tired as I felt.

Colin nodded. "I can also call his attorney and feel him out. Attorneys do that all the time."

"Okay," I whispered. I swallowed through my aching throat. "So I'll be going to Juneau for hearings from this point forward?"

"Yes. They'll offer the option for you to do a live video call, but —"

I cut in quickly. "Absolutely not. I'm appearing in person. I don't want there to be any doubts from the judge that this matters to me."

Colin's phone rang, and his eyes flicked to the phone screen. "Unfortunately, I need to take this call," he said softly.

"Go ahead. Thank you for keeping me updated."

I walked out of his office quickly. I felt stripped raw. I was so cold, it felt as if I was standing out in an icy wind in the middle of the winter without anything on. I often felt cold when it came to anything to do with my ex.

I just needed a few minutes to pull myself together. While I stood there, temporarily frozen in place, the door to the reception area opened. I glanced over to see Adam walking in. I wasn't crying, and I wasn't shaking, but the second his eyes locked with mine, it felt as if he could see straight through all of my defenses. I had some military-grade barricades built up around me, so that was saying something.

Along with all of the hell that came with being in an emotionally abusive relationship, I learned how to hide it from everyone. I'd never wanted anyone who cared about me to know how stupid I'd been.

Quinn happened to be walking out of her office a second later. Her eyes bounced from me to Adam and back again. She knew me well enough to know the blank look on my face didn't bode well for my state of mind. She also knew that I would be here to meet with Colin.

Her eyes arced back to Adam. Even though I hadn't said one word to anyone about Adam, it was as if Quinn put all the pieces together quickly.

"I'm just leaving. If you need my office, it's yours," she said. After she started walking, she stopped in front of me, placing her hand on my shoulder. "I'll see you tomorrow evening, right?"

I had to scramble mentally to remember what she was talking about. "Oh right. Dinner. My place. Yes."

"Perfect." Her touch was comforting and grounded me a little.

She glanced toward Adam. "I forgot about our meeting. We'll have to try another time."

Adam held her gaze for a moment, and I realized he was probably supposed to be meeting with her because Quinn headed up the legal division at Fireweed Industries. Her cousin, Colin, handled the family law cases.

She looked back toward me. "Fireweed Industries. They always need something."

A smile played at the corners of Adam's mouth. "No worries. Catch up with you tomorrow at the office?"

She flashed a smile. "Always."

He held the door for her. Quinn was gone in a blink, leaving Adam and I standing alone in the reception area of an office building where neither of us worked.

Adam didn't hesitate, striding past me and walking into Quinn's office as if he owned it. But then, Adam had that kind of confidence. He was understated and quiet, yet never arrogant. He simply commanded any situation when the moment called for it.

I was still frozen a few feet from Quinn's office door. Adam waited. "You look like you could use a minute. I can leave if that would help."

"Please don't," I whispered, that small request slipping out unbidden.

When my eyes locked with his, my legs were galvanized into motion. I followed him into Quinn's office. It was familiar as I often stopped by to chat with my friend after meeting with Colin.

Only after Adam closed the door and we were in her quiet office alone did everything that I had kept swaddled tight inside begin to break loose. I trembled so hard my teeth chattered.

I felt Adam stopping in front of me, and one of his hands landed on my shoulder. "Do you want me to go?"

I shook my head, and something like a sob came out. Without a word, Adam folded me into his embrace. He was strong and warm, and I simply let him envelop me. I was so cold and tired, so very, very tired.

My sobs weren't big and dramatic. They were slow and soft and sounded as weary as I felt.

Adam murmured soothing sounds while he held me securely against him. One palm began to move in slow passes up and down my back. His touch eased the tension spinning madly inside. Gradually, my sobs and the tears wicking up from my throat slowed. I could take a deep breath, and the shivering and trembling finally stopped.

I honestly didn't know how long he held me in Quinn's office. I felt a little sheepish, but my anxiety was dissipating. I scrambled inside to find my composure. I took a few deep breaths and finally lifted my head.

Adam still held me close, and I loved the feeling. He was warm, and I could've stayed here forever in his arms. He lifted a hand, swiping the tears off each cheek with his thumb. My heart felt cracked wide open.

"Do you want to talk about it?" he asked gently.

It didn't escape me that he didn't ask me what happened. Instead, his question put the control in my hands. I didn't feel like I had to explain.

I contemplated it for a moment. While I didn't want to tell him about the relentlessly badgering process of having my ex use the custody situation as yet another way to make me miserable, I did want to explain some of it.

"Rich is filing for shared custody. This should be good because, until today, he has been demanding full physical custody. But he wants shared legal custody and for me to keep physical custody. That means we have to make decisions together, and he wants us to attend co-parenting classes. Together! I don't want to be forced into that with him. I also know he doesn't really want custody. He just wants to make my life a living hell."

Adam quietly absorbed what I'd shared, his expression calm. After a beat, he nodded, just barely. "Rich is a fucking asshole, but you already knew that. I know you're a fighter, Tessa, because you left and divorced him. Just remember that. If you ever need anything from me related to this, I'll help however I can. All you have to do is ask."

That was all he said. Yet I was instantly calm. A part of me had surrendered already. I would have these moments when I felt like I couldn't control my anxiety, but then I would remember that the one thing I could control was my own response. I had already done the hardest part. I'd left.

That was the wildest part, the paradox of getting caught in this dynamic. When I felt like I was falling apart and weak and at the mercy of someone else, the experience of that helped me become stronger. The strength I got from that carried me through. I just had to remember to reach for it.

I took a slow, steadying breath. "Thank you," I said, my voice soft.

Adam nodded. After a few beats of quiet, he dipped his head, surprising me with a kiss. This comforting kiss lingered. A moment later, he eased his hold on me and stepped back. Every movement was purposeful and deliberate.

"Should I walk you to your car?"

At my nod, he turned, opening the office door and gesturing me through. I wanted him to reach for my hand, but he did one better. He placed his palm lightly on my waist, and his touch was like a hot brand.

I felt protected with every step. He walked me to my car, opened the door, and waited until I buckled up.

"Call or text anytime."

Chapter Six

ADAM

That evening, I found myself turning on the TV to watch the weather report. More specifically, to watch Tessa.

My lips curled at the corners the moment they announced, "And here is Fireweed Harbor's very own Tessa Hensen with our evening weather report."

Tessa smiled at the camera and began reporting the weather. I didn't pay much attention to the details, but she was perfect. Toward the end, there was an educational segment that had started since she had begun doing this forecast. Tonight, I learned the difference between two types of clouds.

After they shifted away from the weather, the next segment discussed this summer's fishing season. My thoughts zoomed right back to this afternoon.

I wanted, to the point of cold fury, to do something about Tessa's ex. But I knew there was nothing I could do beyond trying to be there for her. Today, I'd resisted the urge to walk back into the attorney's offices to talk to Colin Blackthorn. He was a friend of sorts. I also wanted to talk to Quinn about it.

But I knew Tessa wouldn't likely appreciate me doing that. I imagined she was accustomed to having so many details of her life orchestrated by her ex. I was accustomed to managing things and solving problems. Yet I also knew well how to stay out of the way. In my own family, Kenan and I had played the peacekeepers for the most part. We adopted that role differently.

Restless, I entered the kitchen and opened the refrigerator, only to discover what I already knew. It was almost empty.

I lifted my phone and called in a take-out order from Fireweed Winery. I tossed my phone back on the counter and glanced around. Kenan and my other brothers helped me build this place.

My house was bigger than I needed, but I was too practical not to consider resale value even though I didn't intend to move. The house was just beyond the main downtown area of Fireweed Harbor along one of the bluffs that overlooked the harbor. The kitchen was to the back, beyond the open area living room. With it being summer, the sun was just setting even though it was already late evening.

The light-colored hardwood floors gleamed under the late evening sun as it slid down toward the mountain range. The flooring shifted to tile in the kitchen area with a bathroom and laundry area at the back. Stairs led up to a loft, where I had an office. That area also had a view with the desk built into the railing along the upper floor. The main bedroom was on one side upstairs, and a short hallway with two more bedrooms was on the other side.

I began to pace with restless energy buzzing through me. *I could always work*, I told myself. I had the desk upstairs and did work there, but I worked as much downstairs on my laptop on the sectional in the living room area or on the island in the kitchen.

Just as I was about to jog out to my car to pull my laptop out of its bag, my phone vibrated on the counter. I spun it around, and my heart started kicking hard against my ribs as soon as I saw the text.

Tessa: *Can I see you tonight?*

I didn't even hesitate. I lifted the phone, tapping the screen to slide open her text and reply.

Me: *Absolutely. Should I pick you up?*
Tessa: *Please.*

I jogged out to my car seconds later, calling the restaurant to change my order to a pick-up. I called Tessa a moment later. "I already ordered takeout. Do you want anything?"

"Uh, sure," she said, sounding a little surprised.

"What would you like?"

"Um, what did you get?"

"The chicken curry special."

"I'll take the same. I love that one."

"You got it."

"I'll get you first, and then we'll go pick up the food together."

When Tessa hesitated, I shifted gears. "Or I'll get the food and come get you."

"That would be great," she said quickly.

"See you in a few."

I called the restaurant to add to my order. I waited impatiently when I got to the restaurant.

Tessa had texted me her address, which, uncharacteristically for me, I hadn't even thought to ask for. I didn't know where she lived because, well, I hadn't paid much attention to Tessa until a week ago. And now, she was practically all I thought about.

Anticipation sizzled through me like little streaks of lightning across the sky before a storm. Tessa had specifically instructed me to come around the back with a follow-up text.

I suspected I knew why but didn't want to contemplate it tonight. Her house was a small A-frame-style home. I recognized it as one rented through our family's property management company. I suspected her ex had fought to keep whatever house they had shared in the divorce.

She was opening the back door before I even got out of my SUV. I watched as she turned and checked to make sure the door was locked behind her.

"Your lights are on," I commented as she jogged down the stairs.

She didn't even look back over her shoulder. "I know."

When she stopped in front of me, I wanted to kiss her. A light, giddy sense was inside me as if a warm breeze gusted through my heart.

I shackled the urge. I noticed her glancing around as if she were worried someone was watching.

Once we were in the SUV and I was driving, I slid my gaze to hers. "How are you?"

"Better than when you saw me this afternoon." Her tone was matter-of-fact, and I remembered the feel of her trembling in my arms. "I mean, the bar is low." Her tone was dry, and the laugh that rustled in her throat contained a bitter tinge.

"What do you mean?"

"I mean falling apart after meeting with my lawyer and having a breakdown in public. That's all. Can we not talk about that? I shouldn't have even said anything."

The stop sign ahead was convenient. Once I came to a full stop, I turned to look at her. "You can say whatever you want. If you want to talk about it, you can. If you don't want to talk about it, you can also do that. I was just asking how you were."

She held my gaze and took a quick breath. "My life is kind of a hot mess. I'm not so sure you want to deal with it."

"It's no messier than anyone else's, Tessa. I don't say that to belittle how you're doing. It's just everybody's life is a little bit messy. I want to deal with you and whatever comes with you," I said, my tone clear and definitive.

"Okay." Her voice was just above a whisper. Yet again, the urge to kiss her was almost overwhelming.

A horn honked behind us, and I yanked my eyes away from hers and began driving again. A few minutes later, I turned into my driveway.

"This is so pretty!" Tessa exclaimed.

"I can't take credit for the landscape since that's nature's doing, but I designed and built the house myself with help from my brothers, of course."

"Must be nice," she said as I tapped the remote to open my garage.

"What's nice?"

"Having that many siblings. You always have someone to turn to."

Until these recent events, I'd never wondered if Tessa had siblings. I knew she'd grown up in Fireweed Harbor, but that was it.

Before pondering that further, I answered, "Sometimes I wish it was just me in the world, speaking of messy. Then there are other times I can't imagine life without my siblings. They tend to be..." I contemplated my choice of words. "Over-involved."

Tessa snorted as I put my SUV in park and tapped to close the garage door behind us.

"There's a lot of love there," she offered.

I glanced over at her as I reached between the seats for the bag of takeout in the back seat. Her scent drifted to me. She smelled fresh, almost like a spring breeze.

Once again, I resisted the urge to kiss her. It was an almost constant need, an insistent knock on the door of my body.

As we climbed out together, I finally assuaged my curiosity. "You know, I don't even know if you have siblings."

"What do you know about me?" She stopped beside me as I tapped in the code on my door before walking into my kitchen.

"I know you're my sister's friend, and you were just young enough when we were growing up that I didn't pay a lot of attention to you. And, of course, you probably know this from McKenna, but things are a little messy in our family."

My measured statement belied the roiling anxiety and dread that had colored most of my childhood after our father passed away unexpectedly.

"I do know that from McKenna. It's just me and my parents. I love my parents, and they're still together. I'm close to my uncle David."

"Ah, yes. I knew David was your uncle." David had been the chef for our restaurant for many years until recently shifting to admin duties only.

We were in my kitchen now, and I set the takeout on the counter. Tessa had stopped beside me and was looking around. "It's beautiful inside too." Her gaze completed its arc about the space before reaching mine again.

"Thank you." I paused as a sense of uncertainty started to unspool inside. I wasn't used to feeling this way. I kept things so, well, so impersonal.

She idly rubbed her fingers along the hem of her shirt. The urge to tug her into my arms and hold her close was almost overpowering.

I usually thought everything through—numbers, details, and so on. I wasn't thinking when I stepped closer and reached for her hand. I was gratified when she instantly curled her fingers into mine.

"Are you nervous?" I asked.

She started to say something and paused before shaking her head, as if to herself. "Yes." She took a quick breath. "It's not you. It's the situation."

"What would help you feel better?"

She stared up at me, pink staining her cheeks.

"Kiss me," she whispered.

"All you had to do was ask."

I moved a little closer. I lifted a hand to palm her cheek and slipped my other arm around her waist. I looked into her eyes for a long moment, giving her time.

"Are you sure?" I whispered over her lips.

Chapter Seven

TESSA

Are you sure?

I felt the shape of Adam's words on my lips. My racing pulse galloped along so fast I could hardly breathe. I felt liquid heat pool low in my belly, and I was acutely aware of the throb of need at the apex of my thighs.

My nerves felt stretched tight, shimmering with sparks. I couldn't focus on anything but Adam. All of my attention centered on my body's humming drive to lose myself in him.

"Yes," I whispered.

Before that single syllable fully crossed my lips, he fit his mouth over mine. His hands slid into my hair. I shivered at the way he took control of our kiss. He angled my head to the side, his tongue sweeping in masterful strokes against mine. I arched into him, needing this kiss, needing his strength, needing to lose myself in the flames of this fire.

I had no idea how long our kiss lasted, but when his lips lifted away, I heard myself whimper, bereft to lose him. His hand slid away from my hair, the other sliding from where it rested between my shoulder blades down my side. He gripped my hips and lifted me onto the kitchen counter.

He pressed hot, open-mouthed kisses along the underside of my jaw. Each one felt like a drop of lava on my skin, ramping the heat up inside.

"It's okay," he whispered against my skin. "I have you. I'm not going anywhere."

I'd never had faith in any man. I'd thought myself incapable of experiencing that with anyone. Yet with Adam, I did.

I was the first to seek something more than the fabric between us. My hand found its way under the hem of his shirt to discover his warm skin. He felt alive and shimmering. He was muscled and lean, and I let my fingertips walk up his chest, savoring the soft crinkle of hair under my touch. I let my palm press over the resounding beat of his heart.

Discovering his pulse raced as rapidly as mine was a relief.

He lifted his head. "Tessa." My name was a gruff whisper.

I dragged my eyes open. My legs dangled off the counter, and my hips rested at the edge, where I could feel his hot, hard length nestled against me.

This moment felt intensely carnal even though we were fully clothed. His gaze was dark and laser-focused on me.

"Maybe we should stop," he said.

I shook my head fiercely. "No."

His eyes widened slightly. I could feel the press of his fingertips on one of my hips through the fabric of my soft cotton pants.

He moved his hand and placed it on the counter beside me. A small sound of protest came from my throat.

"Tell me what you want," he said softly. "We don't have to rush. I'll wait for you, wait until you're ready for more."

While I appreciated him being courteous and patient, I was no virgin. I hadn't had an orgasm with a man in... Well, ever. My ex was the only man I'd been with. Sex with him had been filled with tension and critiqued to the point that it removed any potential for me to relax and enjoy myself.

I took a breath, narrowing my eyes. "I want you. I want this. You don't need to treat me like I'm fragile because I'm not." Although my voice was raspy, it was strong.

"I know you're not fragile. I just want it to be on your terms."

My palm still rested on his chest, and I slid it between us to boldly stroke his cock. Power surged through me when I felt his pulse under my touch.

"This is on my terms, and I want you. All of you. Tonight."

Adam's nostrils flared with a breath, and his eyes darkened as we stared at each other.

"As you wish," he murmured.

On the heels of another breath, his lips were on mine again, and we tumbled into a messy kiss. He stepped back, easing me off the counter, but I tugged him close. He paused, looking down. "I thought we could go to my bedroom."

"I like the counter," I insisted.

I didn't even know what had come over me. But I felt safe and comfortable and downright wild with him. His bed could wait. I'd never had sex in the kitchen. I wanted Adam to fuck me right here on his counter so that every time he walked into this room, maybe he would remember.

His lips kicked up slightly at one corner. My belly shimmied, and desire surged through me like liquid electricity.

"Whatever you want, sweetheart."

I wanted our clothes out of the way. They were nothing more than a hindrance. With his eyes on me, I reached down, catching the hem of my shirt and lifting it over my head in an arc. I heard it crumple to the floor as he sucked his breath in through his teeth. Seconds later, he slid my pants down over my hips. I stood before him in a pair of panties and a bra. They didn't even match, and I didn't even care.

For a split second, I felt self-conscious, but then I met his gaze, and the fire flashing there sent heat rushing through me, sparks scattering like pinwheels over the surface of my skin.

He was still fully dressed, and I opened my mouth to say as much, but he reached for me. Once again, I tumbled into his kiss. When we broke apart, I gulped in air. "I want to feel your skin."

His chuckle against my neck sent shivers chasing through me. He stepped back just long enough to hook a hand on his shirt collar behind his neck and tug it over his head. Seconds later, he lifted me onto the counter again. He shoved my panties to the side as his fingers delved into my core. I was so slippery and needy that I cried out. His voice bordered on slurred when he murmured, "Oh, Tessa. You feel good, sweetheart."

"Adam..." I pleaded as he sank two fingers inside, stretching and teasing me.

I felt his mouth close over my nipple. My fingers speared into his hair as I cried out sharply, the sweet sensation arrowing down.

I was near frantic with incoherent cries and ragged breaths while he teased me to the edge of release. I let out a sharp sound of disappointment when he withdrew his fingers. Before I could demand he not stop, he leaned down, pushed my panties farther to the side, and licked into me. I came almost instantly.

With one hand, he pulled my hips closer to the edge of the counter as he made love to me with his mouth and fingers pumping in and out. His tongue teased in lazy, sensual strokes, glancing over my clit again and again. Until I begged, "Adam, please, I need..." I almost didn't even know what I needed. I just needed to relieve the pressure building to an unbearable tightness inside.

He finally gave me what I needed, thrusting his fingers in deeply with his tongue flattening over my clit just before he sucked on it lightly. The pleasure drew to a piercing pain before it broke. Crashing waves rolled through me as I shook and trembled all over. I was still gasping for breath when he withdrew his fingers and straightened. I heard him moving away. Reality slowly flickered into my awareness when I opened my eyes to see him rolling on a condom. His jeans were open, and his hard length jutted out.

He met my eyes. "Are you sure?"

"Please."

He stepped between my knees. Curling one hand around his length, he brought his cock to my entrance. I couldn't look away as I felt the presence of his thick crown, followed by the slow, delicious feel of him filling me.

"Tessa."

I held his gaze as he stepped closer, his chest coming flush against me. I could feel his heartbeat against mine when he said, "I'm going to fuck you."

Chapter Eight

ADAM

I felt nearly intoxicated at the feel of Tessa's slick, clenching channel surrounding me. This whole encounter had spun so far out of my control that I barely clung to awareness.

I kept telling myself that I could hold on and stay under control.

But then she whispered my name. "Adam, please."

I drew back once more, my eyes on hers as I sank inside her again. With her legs wrapped around me, I could feel her orgasm begin to build, rolling into another. Her cry was soft and low when she rippled around me. My own release sizzled like fire. My balls tightened, and I pumped into her once more, long and deep, before I lost all control and my climax snapped through me like lightning. I clung to her, absorbing her shudders as I growled her name.

Awareness slowly flickered into my thoughts as I breathed with her.

When I lifted my head, I was relieved that she looked as shell-shocked as I felt.

———

A short while later, Tessa sat across from me, her feet hooked around the legs of a stool at my kitchen island.

Although my release less than half an hour earlier should've been more than enough to keep the pounding need at bay, I could feel it rising like an impatient force inside me, water running up against a dam.

Tessa's hair was mussed, her cheeks still flushed, and her lips swollen. After we had untangled ourselves, she cursed because she forgot to bring a change of clothes. She was now wearing one of my sweatshirts, and I tried not to think about how much it gratified me to see her in something of mine.

I'd been hungry before I picked her up, and now I was downright ravenous. I finished chewing a bite of my curry.

"Tell me about your son." I surprised myself with that, but my curiosity about her grew by leaps and bounds. I wanted to know *all* of the things about Tessa.

My prior lack of curiosity about her was shocking to me now. But maybe not. Maybe I just needed the right moment to bring my attention to her.

"His name is Eric." Her eyes twinkled as she cast me a small smile. "Well, you probably knew that."

I narrowed my eyes. "I did, but cut me some slack here. You know how it is when you're younger. Four years was close to forever. I left for college and then went to Seattle before we moved our headquarters back to Alaska."

Tessa shrugged. "We were. Just teasing. Eric is basically the center of my universe. He's with me most of the time, except every other weekend." I could see the shadows chasing through her gaze. "He'll be with Rich until tomorrow."

"What's Eric like?" I prompted.

"He's smart, he's funny, he's kind. He worries about me, and I wish he didn't. There are days when I wish I had never gone on that first date with Rich. But then, as awful as things were with him and probably will be forever because we have a child together, I wouldn't trade him for the world."

Her words were solemn, spoken like a vow.

"Of course you wouldn't." I paused when she took a swallow of water. "I watch your weather forecast," I blurted.

Her eyes lit up. "I love my job," she said so fervently that it instantly curled my lips into a smile.

"You're great at it. I'm sure the schools love your whole educational piece."

She laughed softly. "That happened by accident when I attended job day at the elementary school in town where I used to teach. They had lots of questions, and we started answering them on air. It's fun." She cocked her head to the side. "I'm surprised you watch the weather."

I held her gaze while heat fired inside. "I enjoy watching *you* do the weather report."

"Are we seriously doing this?"

"Doing what?"

"Asking each other about ourselves," she clarified.

"Maybe we know each other already, but I want to know more about you."

She eyed me, her gaze cautious but curious. "Okay. Tell me something about you that I wouldn't already know."

Chapter Nine

TESSA

Adam sat across from me at his kitchen island, where he had just fucked me senseless. I was trying to ignore *that* hot little detail.

He was downright endearing in a way I didn't expect. His hair was tousled, probably from me grabbing onto it when he gave me the first of two intense orgasms. He wore a faded T-shirt that clung lovingly to his broad shoulders and muscled chest. He took a swallow of water as he contemplated my request.

As he studied me, it struck me that, of course, I knew him. I'd been friends with McKenna since we were in elementary school. We'd both been born and raised here. Yet Adam's observation was accurate. He'd been just far enough ahead of me in age that I didn't know him beyond the surface. I knew the broad strokes of their family history and likely some extra details because of my close friendship with McKenna, but I didn't *know* Adam. He was more like a friendly acquaintance.

"I love Steely Dan," he offered.

"Oh, you do?"

"I love '80s music in general," he said somberly although there was a glint of humor in his gaze.

"Really?" I prompted.

"Really. Even before it got trendy again."

"Well, the eighties had some amazing music. I love that era too," I replied.

"Tell me something I don't know about you," he added.

I was discovering something about Adam that I liked. A lot. He was patient. I never sensed he was restless for me to answer. He actually listened. Having only one relationship that was a sheer disaster, I was accustomed to Rich's impatience, his constant annoyance for me to hurry up with what I was saying, or just completely ignoring me. It had gone that way for so long that I shut down and didn't expect to share anything with him. It was easier for me to stay quiet.

I fidgeted in my seat and took a quick swallow of water. "I don't know what you don't know."

Adam rested his elbows on the counter. "In all honesty, I don't know much about you, Tessa. You've been McKenna's friend for as long as I can recall. I know David is your uncle, and I know you married an abusive asshole and had a son. I also know you're a weather reporter and really good at your job."

I could feel the heat rising to the surface of my skin and knew my cheeks were pink. "Oh." I swallowed nervously. "I also love Taylor Swift."

"Well, Taylor Swift is a total badass. She's an incredible songwriter and musician," Adam said with a nod of respect.

"She is. I'm glad you agree," I said with a grin.

"Your turn," I prompted. "What do you do in your spare time?"

Adam was quiet for a few beats, and I could've sworn I saw shadows drift through his gaze like clouds passing across the sun. "I work a lot. I don't have much spare time," he offered quietly.

"I know. But surely you have something you like to do. A hobby?"

"I like to build things."

"Like your house?" I lifted a hand, gesturing in a little circle.

"Yeah, like that. What about you? What do you do in your spare time?"

His question gave me pause because I didn't do much for fun. I could chalk it up to being a mom, which was partially true. But being married to Rich had taken so much from me. He had an opinion about everything, usually negative. To protect myself, I didn't do much of anything because it limited what he could critique about me. As I contemplated this, a piece of knowledge about Adam and me clicked into place.

I knew his family story. I understood he had things to protect himself from, just like I did. I sensed perhaps I trusted him so easily because he understood something that I didn't fully comprehend about myself until this very second. I protected myself so thoroughly.

As we sat there, looking at each other quietly, comprehension flickered between us. It was more than just concrete information. It was unspoken, but I knew he understood it. Precisely as I did.

"I don't have any hobbies. I'm a mom, and I..." I took a quick breath. "I like to read. Maybe we should find some hobbies."

Adam's brows rose. "We?"

"I don't mean together," I said in a rush.

"But it could be," he said quietly. "If you wanted a hobby, what would it be?"

"I always wanted to take cooking classes for things I've never tried."

"Let's do it."

"Together?" I asked, unable to keep the skepticism out of my voice.

"Sure. Do you have a preference? Thai food, Indian food, or something else?"

I pondered this before shrugging and casting him a sheepish smile. "No. Just something new."

"I know there are cooking classes in Fireweed Harbor through the local community school program," he suggested.

"It can't be in Fireweed Harbor," I said quickly.

Adam fell quiet, his gaze measuring. "I think I know why not, but can you tell me?"

"Because if Rich sees me going, he'll start showing up and ruin it."

"What if we didn't let him ruin it?"

"It's not about me," I whispered through the tightness in my chest. "It's about Eric. If Rich is upset with me, he makes things worse for Eric."

"Ah, okay. So we find a class in Juneau."

"I can't fly there for classes!"

"We have company group flight passes. You can go with me anytime. I'm pretty sure Rich can't start monitoring the flights to Juneau," Adam offered dryly.

The flight to Juneau from Fireweed Harbor was twenty minutes. "Really? You would do that?"

"Of course."

I took a shaky breath. "That would be amazing."

"Find a class and sign us up."

The calm confidence in his eyes soothed me. "Does it matter when?"

"I'll make it work. For work, I can usually move things around, work from home, or work late. It doesn't matter."

My heart fluttered, and a sense of surprising joy rose inside me. My cheeks hurt from my smile.

Chapter Ten

ADAM

As Tessa beamed at me, my heart kicked harder and faster in my chest. "So we're going to take cooking classes together?" I prompted.

She waggled her brows. "We are. It's going to be fun. We're both going to learn something."

I lifted my almost-empty bottle of beer. She held hers up, and we clicked them together. I found myself internally stumbling a little. I wanted to linger in the moment, and that wasn't something I often felt.

Her cheeks started to go pink again, but she looked down and quickly stood from her stool. "I'll clean up."

Reluctantly, I followed her lead, and we

quietly folded up the empty take-out boxes to put in the recycling bin. Tessa insisted she needed to rinse our plates.

She turned, her hand resting on the counter. "So should I—"

"Stay." That single word slipped right out before I could think it through.

"For the night?" Her eyes widened.

"Please."

We studied each other before she nodded, just once. She glanced at her watch. "What do you normally do before you go to bed?"

"I watch a show and usually work on my laptop."

"Let's watch something. What do you normally watch?"

"Well, for the past week or so, it's been the weather report. I'm really into it," I teased.

Her lips pressed together as her eyes twinkled with warmth. "What else?"

"I have a few favorites, *Schitt's Creek*, *Ted Lasso*, *The Office*, any of the crime shows where they solve it in one episode."

Her eyes brightened. "I like all those shows. They're good to rewatch. They're comfort shows."

"You choose. I'll watch any of them."

"Well, which streaming service do you have? Because they're not all on the same one."

"I have them all."

"Of course you do. I take turns with them," she said.

"I probably should too."

"Let's go with *The Office*. It's been a minute since I saw that," she finally said.

And so I found myself plunking on the couch with Tessa. Her gaze scanned the living room. "I don't know where your bedroom is. Do you usually watch in here?"

"It's probably not ideal, but usually in my bedroom. I work and stop when I'm sleepy."

"You know that's not great for your sleep," she said pointedly.

"I know. I've never been a good sleeper, though." I shrugged.

"Let's go to your bedroom." Her cheeks flushed pink again, and I loved it.

A few minutes later, we were propped up in my bed. Tessa had insisted on making popcorn. Surprisingly, I had some on hand because McKenna had given me a gift basket of various gourmet microwave popcorn for the holidays.

Tessa had recognized the selection immediately because she got the same thing. "We can tease McKenna for her lack of creativity," she had said when she was putting the bag in the microwave before spinning around. "Wait, no! Don't say anything about us!"

I held both hands up in surrender. "No worries. McKenna would never let me hear the end of it if she knew about us."

Maybe an hour later, when Tessa dozed off curled up on the pillows beside me, I looked over at her. *This can't be serious. You have to keep this uncomplicated.*

But you asked her to stay, my cynical mind lobbed back, pointing out the obvious.

I hadn't spent the night with anyone since college.

I climbed out of bed, careful not to wake Tessa. I tossed the empty popcorn bag in the trash, turned out the lights in the kitchen, and returned to my bedroom. Tessa was sleeping soundly. After a quick stop in the bathroom, I slipped back into bed and lifted the lightweight down comforter up over her shoulders.

I turned off the light and lay in the darkness for a few minutes, my thoughts churning. When Tessa shifted and snuggled close to my shoulder, a familiar tightness in my chest eased. Moments later, I fell into a deep sleep.

———

Something woke me. As my mind pushed through the layers of sleep, I sensed something different. Usually, when I woke up, it was with a jolt.

I was deeply relaxed. When my brain started to flicker online and catalog the sensation of Tessa against me, I discovered I was deeply aroused.

I was spooned around her with her bottom nestled against my aching cock. Waking up this turned-on was new for me.

I took a slow breath, telling my body to stand down. But Tessa wiggled, pressing her luscious bottom against my arousal. I felt her breathing shift and knew she was awake.

"You can ignore that." My voice was rough from sleep.

"What if I don't want to?" she whispered.

I sucked in another breath and buried my face in the sweet curve of her neck, inhaling her scent. She was warm and smelled a little sweet and a little musky.

I let out a low groan, unable to keep my hips from rolling against her when she shimmied her bottom against me again.

"Tessa," I rasped.

"What?" Her voice was velvety soft from

sleep and a little husky. I could hear the hint of laughter in her tone.

Fuck me.

I slid my hand around and up and under her T-shirt. Well, *my* T-shirt. I didn't want to think about how much I loved seeing her in my shirt last night. I slid my palm up over the sweet curve of her belly and trailed my knuckles along the underside of her breasts before cupping one and teasing my thumb over the ruched nipple.

She let out this satisfied little sound in her throat before wiggling her bottom again.

"Tessa," I growled against her neck before nipping lightly.

She shivered, arching into me. "Fuck me, Adam."

Her throaty command was all I needed to slide my palm down, dipping past the elastic band of her panties to cup over her mound and tease my fingers into her folds.

She was slippery wet and made these breathy little sounds that sent lightning in sizzling bolts through me.

"Fuck, Tessa," I groaned.

I could feel cum leaking out of the tip of my cock.

"Fuck *me*, Adam," she clarified with a little giggle.

This version of Tessa—sleepy, sultry, sassy —was enough to bring me to my knees inside. My need, my want, my raw lust for her was a raging bonfire roaring through me.

She shifted a little, bringing her hand up to drag her panties down her legs. I shifted away, reluctantly removing my fingers from where they were buried inside her to get my boxers off.

A moment later, I rocked against her, the underside of my cock sliding along the silky soft skin of her bottom. Somehow, we got her shirt off. I felt almost overtaken. There was no finesse. I wanted, I needed... Tessa.

"Adam..." she pleaded. She pushed her bottom back against me. "I need you."

So much for taking it slow. If she wanted me, she had me.

I reached between us and positioned my cock at her entrance from behind. She shifted to meet me, and I slid in, filling her in one slow surge.

I pressed hot, open kisses on the side of her neck. "Fuck, sweetheart, you feel so good," I slurred.

Tessa shimmied again, and we slowly rocked together. I fucked her deeply. The encounter was intimate and intense.

My own release rushed, whipping through

me. I clung to the edge of my control, sliding my hand down her belly. I circled my fingers over her plump little clit.

"Don't stop," she ordered.

As if I would ever deny her anything.

Chapter Eleven

TESSA

The sweet, sharp pleasure tightened inside me. All of my attention centered on where I could feel the delicious stretch of Adam filling me and his fingers teasing over my clit. I didn't even recognize myself. I was begging, pleading, demanding.

Adam gave me everything I needed. Just then, he gave me the exact amount of pressure, and my pleasure burst through me, my mind going blank with it as I shuddered hard.

I felt his lips on my neck as he filled me once more with a slow, deep pump. I could feel the heat of his release filling me. We trembled together and then lay gasping beside each other, still joined.

I had no idea how much time had passed

when I heard his low, gravelly voice. "I forgot a condom."

I was stunned for a moment. I rolled slightly, angling to look over my shoulder. I could see his face in the dim light cast from a night-light beside the bed.

"I didn't even think about it. It's okay. I promise you don't have to worry about anything with me. I've only been with—" I paused. "One person. And after I found out that he cheated on me, I made sure everything was okay. Also, I'm on the pill."

My heart sped up in an unsteady, nervous beat. Because the whole time I'd been with Rich, he didn't want me to be on birth control. I'd hid my pills from him. I'd actually kept them in my office at work. Just saying it out loud set anxiety kicking up like a storm in my chest.

Adam's eyes held mine in the barely-there light. "Of course I trust you. Considering that I've literally never had sex without a condom in my life until right this minute, I promise we're okay. I should've remembered, and I'm sorry I didn't."

We moved at the same time, and he slipped out of me so I could roll over to face him. "You don't have anything to apologize for. We're both responsible, and we both forgot."

"Okay," he said softly. He smoothed my tangled hair away from my cheek, then leaned close to give me a lingering kiss.

After he drew away, we rested on the pillows, facing each other. Beyond how relaxed I felt, Adam had given me a gift I doubted he could ever understand.

Having never had an orgasm with anyone other than myself, I had wondered if I would ever be able to relax and trust someone enough. He'd shown me that was possible. Maybe this was a small thing that would be a blip in my life, but I would always cherish it. It would be a little memory I kept tucked away.

"What are you thinking?" His low rumbling voice created a subtle vibration inside me.

Our legs were twined together. A little giggle slipped out.

"What's so funny?"

I traced a lazy pattern through the dusting of hair on his chest. "I don't know. This isn't what I expected."

"What did you expect?" he asked.

I took a breath, trying to ease the sneaky

uncertainty that started to slither through me.

"I don't know. Honestly, I just wanted a kiss. This was a lot more than I bargained for."

Adam's fingers were playing with the ends of my curls, and I felt the flat of his thumb smooth across my collarbone. "This was a lot more than I bargained for too."

"What are we going to do now?"

Chapter Twelve

ADAM

There was a sharp knock on my kitchen door. I knew exactly who it was when I heard the door begin to open. I spun around, wearing nothing but a towel wrapped around my waist. My twin brother came striding in. Kenan's eyes widened slightly when he saw me.

"Hey, are you making coffee for me?" he teased.

Before I could tell him to turn around and get the hell out of my kitchen, Tessa came walking out of my bedroom. "Hey, do you know—" Her words sputtered, and her feet slid on the floor as she stopped moving.

Glancing over, I saw her mouth was agape. She snapped it shut. "Hi, Kenan." Her words were clipped.

Kenan looked from me to her. As twins, maybe we couldn't technically read each other's minds, but we could read each other well enough. Thank fuck he sensed I needed him to play it cool and not make too much of this moment.

"Hey, Tessa," he said easily. "I was just dropping off—" He paused. I knew he was formulating some excuse. "The keys to one of the work trucks."

He reached into his jeans pocket, pulled out some keys, and tossed them to me. I caught them with one hand before lifting the mug of coffee in my other hand to take a fortifying swallow.

Just when I thought maybe he would turn around and leave, Tessa spoke. "Please don't say anything. To anyone. Ever."

My brother's gaze flicked from me back to Tessa. "I would never," he said solemnly. "I really have no fucking idea what's going on. Did you have a flat tire or something this morning?"

Considering that I was wearing a towel, and Tessa's curls were damp, her feet were bare, and she was wearing one of my T-shirts that hung to just above her knees, that was so obviously *not* what was going on.

The worried look faded from Tessa's eyes,

and she nodded. "Yes. That's what happened. Adam happened to see me on the road and stopped to help."

"That's Adam. He's a helper," Kenan said with a barely suppressed grin. He cleared his throat. "Well then, I'll be seeing you around." He glanced toward me. "See you at the office later. With that work truck."

"You got it." I knew now that I was, in fact, picking up a work truck for my brother.

With a wave, Kenan was gone. Tessa met my eyes. "Are you really picking up a work truck?"

I smiled. "Now I am. That's my toll."

"Your toll?" She walked into the kitchen, stopping beside the counter and curling one foot over the other. It was so endearing I wanted to kiss her.

"Kenan will keep this quiet no matter what. But he was probably supposed to pick up one of the work trucks today, and I'll do it for him now," I said dryly.

Her lips curled into a small smile. "Oh."

"Coffee?" I gestured to the mug I'd set out for her beside the coffee pot.

"Yes, please. Thank you." She filled her mug and took a few sips.

"No cream or sugar?" I prompted.

"I like my coffee black."

I filed that detail away. I wanted to know *every* little detail about Tessa.

After several sips, she cocked her head to the side. "Are you sure Kenan won't mention this to anyone?"

"I'm positive. We're twins. Even in a family as big as ours, we keep secrets for each other. Am I your dirty secret?" I teased lightly.

She shook her head quickly. "No. I just can't have Rich finding out. Before you go thinking I care about it for myself, I don't. It's for Eric. If Rich makes my life hell, he makes Eric's life even worse. Because that's how he gets back at me."

The resignation in her weary tone made my heart ache. I wanted to fix this for her, but I didn't know how.

"Understood," I said.

We shifted into a mundane conversation. Neither of us mentioned that when we'd woken together, I'd tugged her into the shower with me and fucked her against the tiled wall.

I considered myself a man with discipline and control. Tessa had snatched it away, and I'd never even seen it coming.

TESSA

"So what are we doing?" Adam asked when he dropped me off a little bit later.

"What do you mean?"

"This all started because you wanted a kiss. We're far past that."

I blinked, trying to ignore the blaze of heat in my cheeks.

"Do you want more?"

When I hesitated, he added, "Because I do."

"Yes," I said so fast my cheeks burned even hotter.

His lips quirked at one corner. "How are we going to handle that?"

"Rich can't know. I don't give a shit what

he thinks about it as far as me, but I have to think about Eric."

"I know. I'm pretty good at keeping things quiet. You tell me when and where. If I come to your place, I'll make sure it's not obvious. Do you trust me?"

Chapter Fourteen

TESSA

"He what?!"

"Eric fell. He collided with another player and fell," the Little League baseball coach explained. Her tone was very soothing.

Unfortunately for her, I had no chill. "Is he okay?!"

"He's fine." She remained calm. "He bruised his arm, and he's got quite the scrape on his knee. Now he has tough kid points."

I gritted my teeth. "I'm headed over there right now."

"Eric says he wants to keep playing."

"I'm still coming over."

I ended the call, grabbed my keys, and bolted out the door.

A short eight minutes later, a little dust

kicked up behind my car as I stopped in the parking area for baseball practice.

The coach, Martha, waited for me.

"I figured you'd be here pretty quickly, and you are. Eric's father told me to let you know it's his afternoon for pickup."

My jaw clenched tight enough to crack. Rich had already canceled his visit for tonight, but I didn't want to get into that with Eric's baseball coach.

Instead, I smoothly said, "Okay."

Martha knew to call both of us if something came up at practice. But, like most everyone in town, she had no idea that Rich was a flaming asshole and abusive.

Just then, I heard Eric's voice. "Mom!" I glanced over to see him running toward me, clearly completely fine. As he approached, he stopped and held up his knee. "Look at my scrape!"

I pressed my lips together to keep from laughing. "Looks good."

Martha smiled at us. "You'll wait with him until his dad gets here?"

Eric went still, his smile disappearing instantly. "I thought I was coming with you?"

"We'll see what your dad says when he gets here," I said smoothly, keeping my tone level.

When I caught the look on Martha's face, I realized maybe she understood a little more than I thought.

She rested her hand on Eric's shoulder, giving him an encouraging squeeze. "Eric played great today. We'll see you at practice on Monday."

With a wave, she was gone. Once she was out of earshot, Eric looked up at me. "I don't want to go with Dad. He said when he dropped me off that you were picking me up. What changed?"

It didn't slip past my notice that Eric waited until Martha was clearly out of earshot to say anything. He knew, as well as I did, that people knowing what his dad was really like wouldn't help the situation. My heart twisted with a sharp pain.

"I'm not sure. Let's just see what your dad says when he gets here."

I was relieved that Rich pulled up maybe a minute later. Eric had gone to get his bag from the field.

Rich didn't even get out of his car. He rolled his window down. Before I could even ask what the deal was, he said, "I'm not actually taking him with me. I just wanted to make sure you didn't baby him too much."

I took a quick breath. I didn't even have

to reach for the shields that my nervous system needed to deal with my ex. It was almost a physical sensation of blocking inside.

"He's fine. Do you want to see him?" I asked.

I glanced over my shoulder to see my son walking more slowly, his eyes on the ground. The joy he had had at showing off his scrape for me had been snuffed out at the mere mention of his father. My heart felt scraped as badly as his knee.

Rich called through the window. "Hurry it up!"

I forced myself to breathe slowly through my nose and ignore the anger rising inside.

Eric didn't start running. He had his own little rebellions with his father. I refused to even look at Rich again. Every interaction for him was an opportunity. If I made eye contact, he would scoff and tell me I shouldn't worry so much about my son. He might sneer at Eric for his scrape.

I waited, holding perfectly still until Eric stopped beside me. He lifted his eyes to his dad, holding his gaze without any emotion. "I thought Mom was picking me up."

"She is. Just making sure you weren't being a crybaby," Rich said.

It was remarkable that the insides of my

cheeks weren't bleeding from how often I had to bite them. Eric's expression remained flat. "I'm not."

Rich simply nodded. "See you in two weeks." He rolled his window up.

I stood perfectly still until he had driven away and turned down the road out of sight. I could feel the tension drawn like tight wires inside my body.

Eric reached for my hand. "Let's go, Mom."

I glanced down, and my little boy, the piece of my heart that lived and breathed as a separate human outside of me, was fine. His father's comment didn't even rattle him.

"Are you okay?" I couldn't help but ask.

"I already told you I'm fine."

We walked to my car, and he released my hand, glancing up as I opened the hatch on the back of my small car. "Dad's a jerk. He always will be." Eric shrugged. "I don't care. I'm just glad we don't live there anymore."

My mouth must've dropped open because his brow furrowed. "It's okay, Mom."

I wanted to say so many things, but I didn't. It would do nobody any good, much less me or Eric, for me to dwell on everything I thought I had done wrong. Because the biggest one was ending up with Rich, to begin with. Yet the paradox was that because of Rich, I had my son.

"Are your friends coming over tonight?" Eric asked a few minutes later when we were driving toward home.

I briefly slid my gaze sideways before looking back at the road. "They are."

"I figured. You have them over when I'm supposed to be at Dad's. I like it when they come over. It's fun, and you laugh more than usual."

My heart gave an achy beat, but I ignored it. The bar was low for laughing more when I'd been with Rich.

ADAM

"That'll work." Kenan was across the hallway saying something to Rhys.

I expected him to show up in my office any minute now. He wouldn't be able to resist an opportunity to tease me.

As predicted, a moment later, he crossed the hall and knocked on the inside of my open office door with a grin. "Thanks for picking up that work truck."

"Right on schedule," I returned with a waggle of my brows.

"On schedule?" he prompted.

"Yeah. You showing up in my office."

He shrugged. "Of course. Do you think I'm not gonna show up to give you a little hell?" He glanced over his shoulder before turning back. "What the hell is going on with you and Tessa?"

I looked pointedly past his shoulder to the door. He took a few steps backward and closed it before returning to plunk down in the chair across from my desk. "Well?" he prompted.

I was always honest with Kenan. "I don't fucking know," I said flatly.

"She's one of McKenna's best friends so that could get messy," he pointed out.

I bit back a groan. "I know. Honestly, I don't know what happened. I know her, but I don't really *know* her. She was years behind us in school. The other night, I saw her at the party at McKenna's place and almost kissed her and…"

"A few days later, you took her home and…" Kenan circled his hand in the air.

I let out a sigh as I ran my hands through my hair. "I don't know what I'm doing."

"Dude, you know if you hurt her, McKenna will kick your ass."

I rolled my eyes. "As if I don't know that. Nobody can know. You have to keep your mouth shut about this."

Kenan leveled me with a look. "You know I won't say anything to anyone."

"I know."

He was quiet for a few beats. "Her ex is a fucking piece of work. Total asshole."

"What do you know about him?" I couldn't help but ask.

"Well, you know Quinn does all our legal stuff." Quinn was Kenan's wife, and they'd been best friends for years before they came to their senses and admitted they loved each other.

"Yeah, and what does that have to do with her ex?" I asked slowly.

"Just that I'm at her office pretty often. She's here a lot, but she works at her family's offices too. Her cousin Colin handles all the family cases. I heard him telling Quinn that Tessa's ex would keep her in court for years."

Protectiveness rose swiftly inside me, tension tightening around my chest. "He's a fucking asshole."

"News flash: plenty of men are assholes," Kenan pointed out.

"Remember that girl Rich dated in college?"

My brother nodded. "I do, don't remember her name. I don't know Rich well and don't want to."

I nodded in agreement. "Yeah, he treated her like shit, jealous, controlling, the whole mess." I took a slow breath.

"I haven't thought much about it since, but I remember. She finally dumped him, and he called her all kinds of names. It was ugly," Kenan added.

"Yeah, well, he was worse with Tessa."

Kenan studied me. "This seems like more than just something casual for you."

I narrowed my eyes. "I don't know," I hedged. When his eyes narrowed, I lifted a hand in the air, letting it fall to my desk with a thump. "I don't even know what the fuck is happening. Honestly, I never really noticed Tessa before. Now, I can't *not* notice her, and I can't stop thinking about her."

"She's a single mom. Whatever you do, be aware of what you're walking into," he pointed out.

"I know."

Another silence fell between us. "Do you, though?"

———

Do you, though?

Kenan's question repeated in my thoughts. I thought I knew. Growing up in a big family, we were accustomed to the push and pull of somebody always needing something.

Kenan and I were in the middle of the pack with our other set of twins. I knew what it was like to have a single mom. And holy hell, we'd paid a bitter price for our mom being overwhelmed. Our grandparents helped, which meant years of our grandfather's verbal and emotional abuse, with our oldest brothers being subjected to the worst. We all paid the price. To this day, I wondered how he had treated our father. Our dad had been an only child, and so had our mother. That was why they'd wanted a big family.

Kenan's comment should've given me pause, yet it didn't. It was late in the evening, nothing unusual for me. I was often the last person to leave our offices. I enjoyed the quiet after-business hours.

Without letting myself dwell, I reached for my phone. Tapping the screen to life, I pulled up Tessa's contact. My lips unconsciously curled into a smile.

Me: *What are you doing tonight?*

I felt like I was back in high school when Julie and I used to text. I wanted to wait and see how quickly Tessa would respond.

I forced myself to push my phone away, chuckling as I leaned back in my desk chair.

Dude, she's a grown-ass woman and a mother. She's not sitting around, staring at her phone screen.

I had been reduced to this, with thoughts circling in my brain while I waited in my office at night. I forced my focus back to my computer screen, where I was reviewing reports from our new renewable resources division. We were winding down fossil fuel projects and shifting to renewable energy development. As the CFO, any new projects meant I constantly checked numbers.

When my phone vibrated a few minutes later, I practically lunged for it.

Tessa: *Having dinner with friends. Your sister, me, Haven, Rosie, and sometimes Fiona do this at least once a month. It's at my house tonight. What are you doing?*

Me: *Working late.*

I hesitated for a beat, but then I decided to put myself out there.

Me: *I know we said we would keep this quiet, and I will. But I want to see you again. So how do we do that?*

Chapter Sixteen

TESSA

"Be right back. Bathroom break," I said to the room at large.

I hurried from the kitchen into the bathroom. As soon as I closed the door, I leaned against it and took several deep breaths, trying to slow the beat of my rampaging pulse.

I slipped my phone from the pocket of my jeans and glanced at the screen again. Adam wanted to know how we were going to see each other again. Oh. My. God.

I had no idea. We'd had a brief conversation about it after our unexpected, shockingly intimate, and intensely pleasurable night together.

I pushed away from the door and put the

phone back in my pocket, turning on the cold water at the sink. I splashed water on my face to cool the heat blazing in my cheeks.

After dabbing my face dry, I studied myself in the mirror. With my slightly wavy hair and big eyes, I looked a touch weary. I hadn't really looked at myself in a while. Maybe it was being a mom, or perhaps it was being in an abusive relationship for too long. No matter the reason, I had simply stopped even thinking about myself as a sexual being.

Yet after one night with a man who'd been in my life for so many years, I felt bracingly alive like a blast of wind had lifted me and dropped me in a new place. Just thinking about the heat contained in Adam's eyes after we kissed sent another wash of heat through me. My mind spun to when he fucked me against the wall in the shower after dryly pointing out that shower sex wasn't all that great unless you stayed out of the water. I was burning up inside.

I slid my phone out of my pocket again and typed a quick reply.

Me: *I don't know.*

I sat on the closed toilet even though I didn't even have to go to the bathroom. Adam's reply came quickly.

Adam: *I can come to you any night. Just tell me what works for you. I promise I'll be quiet.*

A disbelieving laugh slipped out, and I leaned my head back as I took a slow breath.

Quiet? Ha! We'd been anything but the other night.

"What's taking you so long?" A voice came from outside the door. "I have to pee," Haven added.

Heat flashed into my cheeks as if my friend somehow knew I was texting my secret new friends-with-benefits guy. I stood, flushed the toilet for good measure, and washed my hands again.

Me: *I'll text you later.*

Haven waited outside the bathroom, dancing on her feet. "Sorry. My bladder hasn't recovered from having a baby."

"No worries."

I slipped across the hallway to check on Eric. He was situated happily in front of his TV, playing one of his video games. There were so many things to keep track of as a mom, one of them was monitoring your child's online gaming behaviors. I was beyond grateful that Eric was comfortable with me checking on things and liked to read as much as he liked to play video games. McKenna had helped me set up a monitoring program, which Eric didn't care about. I wasn't worried about him. I was worried about other people.

"Hey, Mom," he said without looking away from the screen as his thumbs moved rapidly on the controller.

"Bedtime is in half an hour."

"I know, Mom." He tossed me a quick smile over his shoulder.

I stepped into the room and ruffled his hair quickly before departing to return to the kitchen. When I sat down, Haven followed me into the room and glanced around. "I should get home."

"You're like me when Eric was younger. I found it hard to leave him for much time at all," I offered

Haven cast me a sheepish smile. "I know. I don't like leaving Jake for too long even though I know he's asleep, and Rhys is there, and everything is fine. It's just..." She shrugged.

I gave her a quick hug before she departed. McKenna got up from the table and followed her to the door. "I'm going to head home too."

"Go to your lover boy," Rosie teased with a dismissive wave.

McKenna's cheeks went pink. I grinned. "We all understand. You're in love."

"Dinner at my place next time," she said, lightly squeezing Rosie on the shoulder before she left.

Rosie helped me start to clean up. "I can handle it if you need to go," I said.

She eyed the plates and glasses on the table. "I'd like to help." We began cleaning before she glanced over. "I just have one question."

"What's that?"

"What were you doing at Adam Cannon's house?"

Fireweed Harbor was a small town, complete with the usual gossip that raced through it like tiny flames. There was also the unique situation of being in Alaska and off the road system. You had to take a plane or boat just to get here. We had all the amenities, but the winters were long and dark. Residents were bound more tightly together by the shared experience of living on the edge of the wilderness, the wildness itself its own force, tightening the bonds we already shared.

I loved all those things about my hometown. Although I'd hated them while I was married because I'd been so ashamed and found myself keeping secrets from everyone in my life.

I stared at my friend, feeling my cheeks heat. As much as I loved my friends caring about me and worrying about me and wanting me to be okay, I hadn't even been thinking. Rosie lived right near Adam, which I hadn't thought about the other night.

I scrambled in my thoughts, trying to find something, anything to explain away my presence there.

Rosie pressed her lips together to keep from laughing. I finally sighed. "I don't have a good reason."

She nodded slowly, holding her hand out for me to pass over a plate I'd just finished rinsing. She put it in the dishwasher. "I feel kind of slow, but did you ever have a thing for Adam? I mean, we all know him, but..." She shrugged.

"I know! We've all been friends since we were kids, but Adam was—"

When I paused, Rosie interjected, "Four years older, which is like forever in school. By the time we started high school, he had just graduated. After that, he was in Seattle. We've gotten to know Rhys better because he married Haven. And the other brothers have been around town more. Adam keeps to himself."

"Honestly, I never had a thing for Adam. I

thought he was handsome. The whole freaking family is good-looking." I handed her the last plate, and she put it in the dishwasher before closing it. After I dried my hands, I passed the towel to her.

I turned around, resting my hips on the counter and crossing my arms while I tapped my foot nervously on the floor. "I don't know what happened. At McKenna's dinner party, I went to the bathroom. I came out, and Adam was waiting, and it was just a weird thing. I wanted to kiss him, and I'm pretty sure he was going to kiss me. And—"

I got hot just thinking about it. Rosie fanned in front of my face for me with a laugh, and I rolled my eyes. "Then you spent the night with him," she added.

"Nobody can know," I said hurriedly. "If Rich finds out, he will make my life a living hell. As it is, Eric's a chess piece for him to make moves against me."

"How bad is it with Rich? I was hoping he'd ease up," Rosie said softly.

"Colin suggested that he check with Rich's attorney to see if he'll drop the custody case if I agree to forgo child support. He's not paying anyway."

Her gaze sobered. "I'm sorry. I'd kick Rich's ass for you if you'd let me."

I shook my head quickly. "I appreciate the offer."

"I don't think you need to worry about Adam keeping things quiet. There's a reason none of us know him that well. He lays low. That family is not an easy family to be a part of. So much gossip to ignore. I'm sure he'll understand your situation."

I wasn't sure where she was going with this. "What are you proposing, Rosie?"

"That you have lots of hot sex with Adam," she said, her tone completely serious.

I snorted. "You think that's a good idea?"

"Why not?" She cocked her head to the side. "What do *you* want?"

"Well, lots of hot sex with Adam would be a pretty sweet deal," I admitted.

"Then do it. I won't say a word."

"Yeah, but if you saw me there..." I shrugged.

"I saw you this morning in his SUV. Just come and go in the dark and make sure he understands it's important to keep it quiet."

"What about the rest of our friends?" I honestly didn't care much about what my friends knew, but the more people who knew, the more likely the information would make its way to Rich.

"Oh, even if they guess or actually find

out, we are all vaults." Rosie's words were solemn.

Tears sprang to my eyes. My friends' support when I scraped up the courage to leave Rich was invaluable. "I don't know what I would do without any of you!" I gave her a fierce hug as emotion rushed through me.

Rosie squeezed me before she stepped back, holding my shoulders. "You're okay. You're okay."

The amount of relief I'd experienced just being honest with my friends about what my relationship with Rich had really been like was hard to describe. The secrecy and the shame were another part of the pain and isolation. It made all of it feel even worse.

"I know I am." I took a slow breath.

After years of trying to keep myself together while living under the equivalent of Rich's boot on my throat, I still experienced waves of shame and embarrassment about what had happened. Fear and anxiety stirred up little tornadoes in my life. But when the rushes of emotion passed by, the sense of feeling stuck in a dark, lonely place had disappeared. No matter how hard it was to still deal with Rich around the custody situation, Eric and I were free.

Rosie smiled over at me. "You deserve this," she said firmly.

"Deserve what?"

"A man who makes you blush, who makes you want more. Maybe I'm not that close to Adam, but I know he's a good man."

Chapter Seventeen

TESSA

Do you trust me?

Adam's question after our night together played in my thoughts. I *did* trust him. Completely. The last thing I wanted was for something to go wrong, specifically for Rich to find out.

Yet my desire to see Adam was more powerful than what Rich thought.

I re-read his text.

Adam: *I want to see you.*

Eric was sound asleep in his room. With the blessing of youth, he slept like the dead. Some mornings, it was beyond frustrating to prod him out of bed. On the other hand, I could safely have Adam come over, and Eric would most likely sleep right through it.

My hands were shaky when I tapped out my reply. I wasn't shaky from a bad kind of nervousness but from intense anticipation.

Me: *Come over. Park in the back.*

I waited less than a minute for his response.

Adam: *I'll see you in 10 minutes.*

I leaped out of my chair and zipped around my small apartment. I quickly peeked into Eric's bedroom. He was sound asleep. I closed his door and hurried into the kitchen, tidying it for no good reason. I ran into the bathroom off my bedroom.

I was wearing an old T-shirt and a pair of swingy cotton pants. I definitely didn't have time to change. I ran my fingers through my hair, staring at myself in the mirror and silently swearing.

The light's reflection behind my small house arced across the bedroom wall behind me. I raced to the back door and swung it open before Adam had a chance to knock.

"Hey!" I whispered.

Adam's eyes glinted with humor as his lips curled in a smile. His low and rumbly "hey" reverberated through my amped-up nervous system.

I stepped back, letting him into the

kitchen before closing the door quietly and pressing my back against it. My body felt as if an electric circuit was zipping through it in fiery loops.

Turning to face me, he stepped closer and placed one palm on the door beside my shoulder. He cupped my cheek with his other hand. When his thumb traced along my neck, I shivered.

"I think you're going to tell me we need to be quiet." His voice was barely above a whisper.

My nipples tightened instantly, and heat pooled low in my belly. When he took another step closer, I shifted on my feet, trying to relieve the intense ache building at the apex of my thighs.

"How was your day?" he asked.

It was a simple question. But with his fingers sliding through my hair and brushing along the sensitive skin on the side of my neck, I could hardly breathe, much less focus. I sucked in a gulp of air. "It was good. How was yours?" I choked out.

One of his shoulders lifted in an incremental shrug. "It was fine. I'm not sure what's happened, but I can't stop thinking about you."

My heart gave a tricky little beat in my chest. I didn't know what to do with all the feelings rushing through me. All of this was so unexpected. This man who had walked through my life on the periphery was suddenly centered in it.

"I can't stop thinking about you either," I whispered.

He shifted incrementally closer. I felt the muscled press of his body against mine and felt his arousal, hot and hard, pressing just above where I needed him.

I experienced a surge of power. His desire for me elicited a feeling I'd never imagined. I felt bracingly alive, shimmering with a heady intoxication.

He dipped his head, nipping lightly on my earlobe and sending a jolt of electricity through me. Goose bumps rose on my skin, and my breath came in short pants. I felt the hot shock of his lips on my neck with his open kisses.

"Adam," I rasped.

He lifted his head, and I let out a little whimper of disappointment.

"What is it?" he whispered.

"I want you." My belly shimmied at my raw honesty.

"I'm yours."

Before I lost my mind completely, I managed to say, "We have to go to my bedroom."

"Lead the way."

My knees felt liquid as I gripped his hand. I loved my small apartment for many reasons. The very top reason was having this place was a concrete representation of my escape from Rich. At this moment, I was grateful my bedroom door wasn't far away. Blessedly, it was also on the opposite side of the hallway from my son's bedroom.

Adam didn't need to be told to move quietly. Breathlessly, I dashed across the living room, and he followed with silent, nimble steps. A moment later, I stumbled as we rushed into my bedroom. He steadied my hip with one hand and then turned to close the door quietly.

My breath came in ragged pants. I peered up at him. "We need to be quiet. Eric sleeps well, but—"

"I know."

I reached around him to lock the door. I thanked the stars again that my son was a sound sleeper, but I wasn't going to take the risk he might wake for some reason.

When I turned back, Adam was waiting.

He caught my hand in his, reeling me close. "What do you want now?"

I blinked, feeling the heat rushing through me, the roar of need and desire. I felt bold and reckless again at feeling so linked with him. I placed my palm on his chest as I leaned up, answering him with a kiss.

I pressed him back to the wall. Adam didn't miss a beat, letting out a little growl into our kiss. I loved the feel of his strong, protective embrace and the way he held me close. I felt safe rather than overpowered.

I reached between us, sliding my palm over the thick ridge of his arousal. When we broke apart to gulp in air, I swiftly tore open the buttons on his fly, reaching in to curl my hand over his length. I needed more; I needed to feel him. Something was so intoxicating about his desire for me, his need for me.

"Tessa," he murmured against my lips.

"Hmm?" I stepped back just enough to push his jeans and briefs down.

His cock sprang free, and I savored the warm, velvety feel of it as it pulsed under my touch. His head thumped against the wall behind him when I slid my thumb over the drop of pre-cum rolling out. I needed to taste him and lifted my hand to suck the musky, salty tang off my thumb.

His eyes narrowed and darkened. "Tessa," he bit out between gritted teeth

"Mm-hmm?" I leaned down because I couldn't resist. When I brought my lips to his thick crown, pressing an open kiss there, I tilted my head to the side, watching his mouth open slightly as he let out a strangled growl.

Power surged through me. Maybe it was because this was the opposite of how I had experienced any sexual encounter with my ex. I savored the way Adam looked at me. The way I knew I could be free with him, I could be safe with him. All my reserve fell away. I didn't worry if I was going to do this wrong.

I swirled my tongue around the head of his cock before sucking him in and letting my tongue slide up the back of his shaft when I drew upward again. His fingers laced in my hair, giving a slight tug when I sucked deeply again.

He choked out my name in a slurred voice. I settled in to tease him, curling my palm around the base of his cock before drawing back and sucking him in again and again. I felt his body tighten, his hips rocking into my mouth once again.

"Tessa, please," he bit out.

I released him with a pop, leaning back to look up at him.

"I need to be inside you."

I didn't hesitate. When I straightened, his dark eyes stayed locked to mine. I felt liquid all over, my knees wobbly. I took an unsteady breath. Before I could take another breath, his lips were on mine, his kiss instantly commanding. Fiery seconds burned by before he lifted his head, and we sucked in air.

He guided me toward the foot of my bed and turned me, murmuring, "Bend over."

I would've done literally anything he asked at this moment. A moment later, my elbows rested on my bed. I shivered all over at the feel of one of his palms curving over my bottom. He shoved my cotton pants and panties down in one swift motion. His fingers delved between my thighs. I pushed back into his touch when he stretched me with two fingers.

Everything was a new sensation, each one ratcheting the need spinning inside tighter and tighter. The brush of the denim from his jeans on my legs. The feel of his arousal, thick and hot and a little damp from my mouth on the sensitive skin on my thighs.

His fingers pumping in and out. The cool air when he stepped back.

I let out a whimper, bereft at losing his touch even for a few seconds. His palm pressed between my shoulder blades, flattening me on the mattress. With his other hand, he pushed my thighs farther apart just before I felt his mouth on my sex from behind. It was filthy, decadent, and wildly pleasurable as he teased me with his fingers and his tongue.

Within seconds, I was begging. "Adam, Adam, please…"

His reply was low and quiet. "I've got you, sweetheart."

His palm slid around to tease over my clit as he leaned back and pumped his fingers once more. The pleasure crashed hard and fast through me, leaving me trembling all over.

I felt him straighten and gasped at the thick press of his crown at my entrance. The aftershocks of my orgasm were still rolling through me.

"Hurry, please, I need you," I rasped.

"You've got me."

I had to bite my lip to keep from crying out when he filled me. The stretch of him inside was intoxicating. He seated himself deeply in one thrust.

"Come for me again, sweetheart," he whispered as he bent over me, nipping my neck lightly from behind.

I arched into his touch, pleasure racing in a fiery shiver down my spine. I felt the slow pull and slide as he drew back and sank in again. I felt encompassed by him as he curled over me. He reached around me with his fingers teasing over my slippery wet, swollen clit.

On the heels of a shuddering breath and one more deep thrust inside me, I came, the orgasm shaking me to my bones, the pleasure running so deep my knees gave out.

I felt his lips hot against my neck. He filled me once more and began to shudder with me.

The force of my climax stunned me. He was still curled around me, his arm banded around my waist as we tumbled over the edge together.

Several moments later, Adam eased back slowly. "Be right back," he whispered.

I managed to straighten and collapsed on the bed, watching through low-lidded eyes as he returned from the bathroom.

He still had his jeans on when he

stretched out on the bed beside me. He smoothed my hair away from my face, dusting kisses along my collarbone before lifting his head again. "Should I go now?"

My heart thumped hard, and I shook my head before I could think about it.

"Could you stay for a little while?"

Chapter Eighteen

ADAM

Tessa was warm and soft, and I wanted her curled by my side every night, which shocked me. When I thought about that night, now a whopping two weeks prior, and looked into her eyes, it was as if a door into my heart had opened. She walked through, and now she lived there.

I was falling in love with her. I had known her peripherally for as long as I could recall. Even though we hadn't been close all those years, I trusted her completely.

The depth of my emotions floored me. I had honestly never expected sex to be anything beyond a purely physical exchange. I wouldn't call it transactional in the driest sense of the word, but certainly not an emotional experience. There was a woman I'd seen off and on in Seattle over a period of years. I still considered her a good friend and cared about her, but that caring didn't even come close to how I felt about Tessa.

With Tessa, I felt intensely protective. I wanted to slay all her dragons and protect her from anything and anyone who might hurt her. I knew she was strong, strong enough to leave an abusive relationship. I also understood she had to fight her own battles. I wanted to be there to catch her if she fell, to give her more strength if she needed it.

Her fingers traced a meandering path on my chest. I let my hand slide over her silky, soft curls. "When you said a little while, what does that mean?" I cleared my throat.

She lifted her head, her palm flattening on my chest before curling into a little fist where she rested her chin on it. I felt the motion of her shoulder when she shrugged. "I don't know. I mean, you can't be here in the morning." Her mouth twisted to the side. "Mom thing," she added.

"I understand."

I could feel her heartbeat against my rib cage. We were still naked, and she was lying half across me. She took a slow breath. "Like I said, if Rich were to find out, he would make things more difficult than they already are."

"That's a diplomatic way of putting it."

"I don't know how else to talk about it."

"He was abusive. You can just say that."

She blinked, her lashes falling. For a moment, I thought I had gone too far. When she opened her eyes again, there was a sheen of tears there. I let my hand slide down across her hair to curl around her waist and hold her closer.

"I shouldn't have said that," I whispered roughly into her hair.

When I leaned back, she blinked again. "It's okay. I don't often say it like that. Rich's abuse was a secret I kept for years. I still sort of keep it. His parents don't know. Lord knows what he's said to them about me." She chewed on her bottom lip.

"How bad was it?" I asked carefully. I was trying to manage the anger that surged through me and keep it in check.

She let out a little bitter laugh. "It was hell. He didn't hit me often. Four times total. The verbal and emotional stuff was constant. He was angry and irritable. He threw things, he yelled, it was just impossible. There was no way to keep things peaceful. I felt crazy by the end. Totally crazy. And now..." She shrugged. "You saw me at Colin's office. I just get so tired. Rich has filed modifications for custody repeatedly, like ten times, I think. The judge on the case is retiring. He's a family friend of Rich's parents, so it's just made the whole thing worse. We have a new judge in Juneau, and Colin thinks it will help."

"Ten times?" My muscles tightened, and I could feel Tessa tense instantly in response. I forced myself to take a slow breath.

"It's okay," she said quickly. I could hear the wish to soothe my tension away in her tone.

"You don't need to worry about me. I'm upset on your behalf. He's using the court system to keep making your life hell."

I could feel an incremental amount of tension slip out of her when the tightness in her shoulders eased slightly. "He is. Colin says it's an unfortunate tactic. I can handle it. It's nothing like it was living with him."

"Can I help?" I liked to fix things, to make them better. I liked things to make sense in life. That was why I loved numbers so much. Patterns and predictability were built into them.

She studied me before shaking her head.

"I appreciate that you understand. It means more than you could imagine."

"I have some understanding of what that was like for you," I said quietly. The shadow of our grandfather and his harsh, abusive presence loomed large in our family.

"I know you do. I think more people than not understand what it's like. The statistics on abusive relationships are a little shocking."

I nodded as I considered my words. "I want you to know if you need help or are afraid, no matter what happens between us, all you have to do is ask. I'll be there."

Her eyes glimmered with tears. This time, it was me trying to soothe away feelings. "I didn't mean to make you cry," I said hurriedly.

She blinked quickly and shook her head. "You didn't. It's just I don't talk about this much. It's depressing. For me and for anyone else to hear about. It's hard to explain how much it means to know that someone understands."

She dipped her head and pressed a soft kiss in the divot at the base of my throat, the sensation a warm drop of sweet heat. When she lifted her head, she held my gaze for several beats. I experienced a visceral tug on my heart as if threads were being pulled tighter between us.

"What time are you going to leave?" she asked.

"We never did establish how long 'a little while' is," I teased.

Her lips curled in a slow smile, and damn if that didn't create this unfamiliar sense of fizzy joy in my heart.

"Eric usually wakes up early."

"What time do you want me to leave?"

"When it's still dark, but that feels like I'm asking a lot." She bit her lip.

"Not at all. I've never been a great sleeper. I'll probably drowse for a little bit and wake up sometime after midnight. I'll leave then."

"Will you wake me up?" she asked.

"Before I go?"

As she nodded, that unfamiliar sense of protectiveness settled more deeply inside. When she tucked her head into the curve of my neck, I thought I wouldn't fall asleep, but it was easy. I was relaxed with her. When I woke a little while later, I was reluctant to rouse her. But she'd asked me to. At this point, I was starting to discover there wasn't much I wouldn't do for Tessa.

She was still draped partially over me, and I sifted my fingers through her hair, down along her back, and over the sweet, luscious curve of her bottom. She made this little sound in her throat and shimmied closer to me. I felt the soft give of her curves against me when she moved. When her knee brushed the side of my cock, it swelled. Fuck me.

"Tessa," I whispered into the curve of her neck. Even her scent intoxicated me. She smelled a little sweet and salty.

She mumbled something and lifted her head, blinking her sleepy eyes open. Her throaty voice, roughened from sleep, only tightened the sharp claws of need. "Are you leaving?"

"I should." Merely saying that deepened the sense of reluctance I felt.

She surprised me when she shifted and rose to straddle me. My hands fell to her hips when she rocked, sliding her slippery core over the underside of my cock. I could feel cum dripping from the tip onto my abdomen.

"Tessa," I warned.

"Just before you go," she whispered.

I swallowed, scrambling for control. "Sweetheart, just so you know, I don't think I could ever say no to you."

She bit her lip and rocked her hips again. There was no fucking way I could've stopped her. She lifted her hips and reached between us. On the heels of a breath, I curled my palm around my cock, positioned myself at her entrance, and filled her in a swift surge as she sheathed me.

It was fast. She rocked with me, her body tightening within seconds before she began trembling as she rasped my name. My orgasm was beyond intense, shaking me to my very bones.

Moments later, we still trembled. She pressed a palm on my chest and looked down at me. "Thank you for coming over tonight."

"When can I see you again?"

Chapter Nineteen

ADAM

Kenan came striding into my office with nothing more than a sharp knock on the inside edge of the partially open door. He waggled his brows before he turned to close the door behind him. I leaned back in my chair when he sat down across from my desk. "How are you?"

"Fine, you?"

He shrugged. "I'm great."

"Why do I feel like this visit is loaded?"

His grin stretched. "Because I happened to see your SUV headed toward Tessa's place the other night."

"Oh, for fuck's sake." I tapped save on the spreadsheet I was working on before I closed my laptop and leaned back in my chair. "This town isn't exactly big. Just because I was driving near someone's house doesn't mean it has anything to do with them."

My brother's brows hitched up, his gaze skeptical. "I know you. You're not usually driving anywhere at that hour."

I pressed my tongue into my cheek, considering what to say. I actually liked having a twin brother. I always knew I had someone in my corner. The only downside was that he knew me better than anyone, meaning he understood more about me than most people. Even with my other siblings, I could get away with being vague and hedging on certain topics.

I decided to roll with it, though, because I needed his feedback. I drummed my fingertips on the arm of my chair and let out a sharp breath. "This isn't going the way I expected."

"What did you expect?" Instantly, Kenan's gaze shifted from sly and teasing to focused and serious.

I resisted the urge to sigh. "I didn't expect any of this. I thought it was a fluke that night. And now—" I leaned forward, steepling my hands together. "I think it's complicated. I can't believe I'm going to say this, but I feel like I'm all in. And Tessa has no idea."

Kenan tipped his head to the side, studying me quietly. "What do you mean 'all in'?" he asked, complete with air quotes.

My heart kicked unsteadily in my chest. I shook my head, wondering what I meant. "I'm not ready to say I'm in love because, for fuck's sake, it's only been two weeks. But at this point, I think I might do anything for her. You know, take care of her, make her dinner, run errands with her, make her ex's life as hellish as he's made hers. I know she wants me to let her take care of that, and I will because that matters to her."

"That sounds an awful lot like love," Kenan said, his lips kicking up slightly at one corner.

"It's insane, though. I mean, she's been in my life forever because she and McKenna have been friends since—"

"Kindergarten," Kenan offered with a light shrug. "I'm with you. Since Quinn and I got married, I've seen Tessa a lot more because they hang out. It's not like Tessa's some random stranger you never met. If I can fall in love—" My brother tapped his chest with his fist. "So can you. Unlike me, you've had a serious relationship before."

I thought about Julie. "We were young. I don't think we would've lasted. Hell, I know we wouldn't have lasted. She was trying to figure out how to break up with me." Kenan was one of the few people who knew about that.

"You're over that, though," he pointed out.

He was right, and I knew it. It burned a little. That love had been young. I'd wanted something to hold on to, something good. Julie had represented that for me at a time when I needed it.

"I am. I have been. It's just..." I shrugged.

"Our fucking messy family."

We all shared cynicism, anger, and trauma because of our grandfather. We'd dealt with the loss of our father and then our abusive grandfather "helping" because my mom had her hands full. Nobody protected us except maybe Rhys. Jake drank himself to death. And just a few months ago, we had all learned that our oldest brother had physically assaulted and bullied our only sister. That kernel of information had shattered our mother. Although it wasn't like it was a surprise. Maybe Jake hadn't been physically aggressive to the rest of us, but we'd seen his temper. We all had a role in the dance of trauma within our family. Mine and Kenan's had been as the mediators.

"It would be okay," Kenan said softly.

"What would be okay?"

"For you to fall in love."

"Oh, for fuck's sake, I'm not —" My words cut off abruptly as I let out a sigh and ran a hand through my hair.

"She just means a lot to you," Kenan said, his tone bordering on mocking.

"What the hell should I do?"

He studied me. "You knew I was in love with Quinn before I did."

"Yeah, but you two had been good friends for years by that point. This thing with Tessa just isn't the same."

"It never is. Maybe you're not in love yet, but I'd say you're definitely falling. It'll probably be a crash landing, but you'll be okay." The humor faded from his gaze as he leaned forward in his chair. "You are one of the best men I know. Sure, I'm biased because I'm your twin brother, but you are as loyal as they come. You take care of everyone who needs you. You're made for this. I like Tessa. She deserves a man like you."

"I'm coming!" Eric's feet thumped on the floor as he came barreling out of his bedroom, still tugging a T-shirt over his head. He skidded on his socks, spinning to a stop just in front of the small bench by the door, which had cubbies underneath it where we kept our shoes.

Moments later, he had stuffed his feet into his tennis shoes, leaving them untied, of course, and thrown a jacket on. He smiled up at me. "Am I late?"

I waited by the door and glanced at my watch. "You have a full minute to spare. Let's go."

He snatched his backpack off the hook above the cubbies, and we hurried out to my car. In short order, he was dashing into school, while I followed at a slower pace. Eric loved school, and he excelled at it. For that, I was grateful. Today, we had parent-teacher conferences. Rich had demanded that the principal and Eric's homeroom teacher accommodate *his* scheduling needs. Unlike the rest of the universe, who just showed up at the appointed time, Rich badgered and pitched fits until he got what he wanted.

I was early, planning to be seated in the conference room before Rich. That was the only way to avoid a parking lot conversation. I had also asked McKenna to call me, specifically when the meeting was ending, so I could excuse myself and say that I had to take a call for work.

I had barely gotten seated when Rich came walking into the room. Instantly, that familiar cold sense of dread slithered through me. My fingertips felt numb and tingly. My therapist had told me that indicated a vagal nerve response. She explained the physical reactions were almost primal and outside of my control. Her gaze had been concerned when she added, "That's a reflection of how traumatic it is for you to be around him. Your nervous system knows you're not safe when he's near."

I forced myself to breathe through my nose, mentally reminding myself not to react and to stay calm. Rich's gaze was flat when he greeted me.

Eric's homeroom teacher came bustling in. I was beyond relieved to have another adult in the room with me. "Hi!" I said, my voice coming out a little too bright.

The teacher glanced back and forth between us when she sat down. I prayed the principal would show up. It shouldn't have mattered, but the principal was a man, and *that* mattered to Rich. He was more respectful toward men.

Just when I thought the principal wouldn't be here, he walked in. Even though he and I had never spoken of it, I sensed he understood what I was dealing with regarding Rich.

"Rich," he said with a nod before he glanced at me. "Tessa. Nice to see you both." He looked at his watch. "We have fifteen minutes."

Eric's homeroom teacher informed us that he was doing really well in school, which was nothing I didn't already know. Because Rich was a fucking asshole, he asked a bunch of pointless questions. He liked to make it seem like he was really involved when he'd never once helped Eric with homework.

The principal interjected precisely fourteen minutes after the meeting had started. "Your son is in the top percentile of his class. His testing has no areas of weakness, and he has all A's. Is there anything else you need to know?"

Rich narrowed his eyes. "I'd like to see a better performance in sports. He's not excelling in any of them."

My stomach churned, and my fingertips tingled again. I clenched my hands into tight fists under the table before stretching them open, trying to bring warmth into them. I knew Rich wanted Eric to be a sports star like Rich imagined he'd been. To my knowledge, he'd been an average football and baseball player in school, but he made it sound like he'd been amazing and only hadn't gotten scholarships to college due to a minor injury that I was pretty sure he'd fabricated.

The teacher spoke up, bless her freaking heart. "Eric is young. He has plenty of time to grow into his strengths."

The principal nodded and stood. "Well, our time is up. Nice to see you both."

Blessedly, my phone vibrated as planned. "I have a call to take from work," I said, glancing at the screen. "Thank you both." I hurried out without even looking in Rich's direction, dipping into the bathroom in the hallway.

I knew this bathroom had a window offering a narrow view of the parking lot. I could see out there if I stood at an angle. I would wait in here until I watched Rich drive away. These were the crazy things I did to manage my sanity and limit my interactions with my ex-husband. I would never regret having my son, but I would always regret that Rich was his father and that I couldn't change that.

With my eyes trained on the parking lot, I answered the call. "Hey, thanks for calling."

"I consider it my duty as your friend. I will call you whenever you need me to call you," McKenna said firmly. "I'm not going to ask how the meeting went because I know Eric's doing great in school. How are you?"

"I'm fine." I took a breath and let it out slowly.

"You *are* fine." Her warm tone was encouraging.

I felt my lips curl into a smile. It was small, but it was a victory. "I am."

I watched as Rich walked to his car. A moment later, he was driving away while

McKenna was saying something about making sure I came to locals' night.

"Please. Fiona said her mom is babysitting her daughter so you can drop Eric off over there."

"You think that would be okay?"

"She offered, so of course. Her mom is the sweetest."

"I'll text her to confirm. So I'll see you there tonight?"

"Meet me at my office. We can walk over together."

"It's a plan. Thank you again for calling me."

"Anytime. Seriously."

Chapter Twenty-One

TESSA

That evening, I walked into the lobby of Fireweed Industries. Although it was an international corporation, its headquarters here in Fireweed Harbor was unassuming. While it *was* the largest building in town, it was only two stories tall.

I'd been here so many times to meet McKenna. Yet now, my heart started to kick faster because I remembered the other night in Adam's office. I wondered if I would see him.

I wanted him to come over every freaking night for more time with him, more kisses, more *everything*. We'd started to text back and forth frequently.

I walked down the hallway upstairs and

passed by the reception area for the executive offices. "Hey, Tish!" I called over to the receptionist.

She glanced up with a quick smile as she stood from her desk. "Hey. If you're meeting McKenna, she's finishing up a meeting with Haven and a print supplier. They're probably about a half hour behind. She told me to tell you. You can wait here if you'd like. I'm headed out, though." She slipped into her jacket and hurried past me.

Once she was out of sight, I glanced around. Adam's office door was closed. Even so, my pulse began to race with anticipation.

I stopped in front of the door and knocked, wondering if he was here. A moment later, the door opened. Adam's eyes widened slightly.

"Hey," I said breathlessly.

"Come in." He reached for my hand, and I stepped through the door before he closed it behind me.

Before I could say another word, he backed me against it and kissed me. By the time he lifted his head, I had hooked a foot around one of his legs and was rocking my hips against the hard ridge of his arousal. We stared at each other.

"Are you meeting McKenna here?" he

asked. I swallowed and nodded. "How much time do we have?"

"Tish said McKenna had about a half hour left in a meeting."

He reached around me, locking his office door. A moment later, I whimpered when he stepped away.

He led me across his office. My knees were wobbly. My belly trembled, and with every step, I felt the slick friction at the apex of my thighs.

Adam brought me all the way around his desk to the side where his chair was. He pushed it back as I asked, "What are we doing?"

"I'm fucking you on this side of my desk so I can remember it every day when I'm sitting here working," he said bluntly. He came up behind me, nipping my neck.

A gush of moisture soaked my panties. My purse fell to the floor as he reached around me. His hands slid under my shirt, cupping my breasts and pinching my nipples through the silk of my bra.

"Adam," I gasped.

"Right here, sweetheart."

He dragged his hands over my belly, unzipping my jeans before pushing them down around my hips until they banded around my knees. His hands slid up and down my thighs before one reached to cup the front of my mound, his fingers teasing over the wet silk.

"For me?" he whispered when he nipped my ear.

I nodded wordlessly. Because I couldn't even form a single word.

He rocked the hard ridge of his denim-covered cock against my bottom.

I was aroused to the point of delirium. This all felt so naughty. I heard footsteps in the hallway, and my pussy clenched.

"Nobody can come in. Let them knock." His lips moved against my neck, sending goosebumps racing over my skin. He peeled my panties down around my thighs. "Bend over, sweetheart."

He slid a palm up my back, pressing between my shoulder blades with a coaxing touch. I would've done anything he asked, and this was a simple request. I bent over. My shirt rode up his wrist as he slid it up my back. His desk was cool against my skin, a contrast to the heat rising inside me.

He stepped back, dropping hot kisses down my spine. Every place his lips landed made me tremble. His kisses were like hot drops of honey on my skin, the heat sliding through me. He reached a hand between my thighs, pushing them apart a little. I heard him move back.

"Oh, sweetheart, you're so wet." He blew lightly on my sex, and I shivered.

I could literally feel the beat of my heart in my clit. It was swollen and so needy. He licked into my folds from behind, and I cried out, my hands trembling as they gripped the edge of his desk. He began to fuck me with two fingers, and I was near frantic, my hips pressing back.

Before I knew what hit me, I felt his fingers slide up to press against my clit. My climax whipped through me so hard I had to bite my lip to keep from crying out. The sound was a strangled moan.

I was trembling and shuddering when I felt him stand. I heard the sound of a zipper followed by the feel of the velvety skin of his cock between my thighs. He positioned his thick crown at my entrance.

"Do you want me now, sweetheart?"

I could hardly breathe, much less speak. I nodded, savoring the cool wood of his desk against my hot cheek.

Chapter Twenty-Two

ADAM

I looked down at Tessa. She was bent over my desk, her pussy glistening with the plump lips of it nestled around my cock. I was already dripping and on the edge of my release. She was so fucking hot. The little sounds she made, the way she was just there for me and with me.

Her pussy still rippled from her orgasm when she whispered, "Please, Adam..."

When she said my name, all I could do was sink inside her. Her pussy clenched around me. She was slick, and I held still, clinging to my control. I was at her mercy. I curled over her, kissing the side of her neck, then her mouth when she turned her head to the side.

My voice slurred when I said, "Tessa, can you come for me again?"

I rocked my hips, nudging a little deeper inside her. "Yes..." she rasped.

There was so much pressure where we were joined from our position. The way my jeans were just barely shoved down my hips, and her thighs were tight together from her jeans around her knees. I shifted, reaching around her. I felt the hard press of the desk against the back of my hand when I teased my fingers over her needy clit.

My release was almost there, sizzling electricity at the base of my spine. I rocked deeper into her, saying, "Come on, sweetheart, just one more for me."

I gave her just a little pressure when I drew back and filled her in a deep thrust. I buried my face in her hair when she began shuddering, her channel clenching tightly around me. My release slammed through me, filling her in hot spurts.

We rested together on my desk. Slowly, my awareness flickered in. I looked down as I straightened, knowing I would think about this every time I sat at my desk. Her bottom was curved up, her skin pink, and her hair a tumble around her shoulders.

Although this was the hottest fuck of my

life, something so tender and intimate about this moment disarmed me. A few minutes later, I looked down at her after we tidied our clothes.

Her eyes were wide and passion-hazed. I *had* to kiss her again. When I drew away, I startled myself by saying, "I think I'm falling in love with you."

Chapter Twenty-Three

TESSA

I think I'm falling in love with you.

I was still reverberating, physically and emotionally, from my fiery-hot encounter with Adam in his office. Until Adam, I honestly wouldn't have believed that I could experience such sexual moments tangled within a sense of intimacy and tenderness. He stripped me bare and cracked my heart wide open.

I'd been so shocked by his words that I simply stared at him with my mouth falling open.

As if he could see through the fear and anxiety banging like loud drums in my mind and heart, he lifted his knuckles and nudged my chin up. "You don't have to say anything. I know all you wanted was a kiss."

Tears had stung my eyes, not from sadness, but from almost a pure sense of emotion that he could understand how complicated this was for me.

Even then, I'd scrambled for the courage to give him the honesty he had given me.

"I know that's all I wanted to start with, but it's a lot more than that now," I'd finally said.

An elbow nudged me in the side. It felt like a needle scratching on a record in my thoughts. Glancing sideways, I found Rosie looking at me expectantly.

"What?"

Rosie waggled her brows. "You're kind of zoning out." She leaned closer, whispering, "And you're staring at Adam. He's staring back, if you're wondering."

I was relieved by the murmur of voices around us, glasses clinking, and the general commotion as my cheeks heated. "Ohhhh. Am I that obvious?"

"To me," she said dryly.

I pressed my lips together to keep from laughing.

"And heads-up. Over at your ten o'clock. Rich is with someone."

The urge to look in Rich's direction was strong. But I held firm, looking straight ahead. "Um, Rich is here?"

Although locals' night at Fireweed Winery was for anyone, this had felt like my territory. McKenna was my friend, and this was her family's restaurant. Ever since they had moved the corporation's headquarters back to town, the family came out in force for locals' nights. I often accompanied McKenna and our other friends.

Rich used to mock the Cannon family. He would never admit it, but he was so very clearly envious. He also made snide remarks about their "fucked-up" history. Before I'd learned how important it was for me *not* to let him know what I was thinking or feeling, I'd screwed up.

In the heat of an argument, when he was telling me it was stupid to care about my friendship with McKenna, I'd blurted out that he was just jealous of the family and that at least their family wasn't as fucked up as his.

That was one of the times he had hit me. I'd gotten a hard slap on the face and a punch in my gut. It had knocked the breath out of me, and the pain had been intense. Bruising spread along my rib cage in the following days. That had been the last time that I ever let myself blurt anything out. As Rich said another time in the future, I had to learn my lesson.

I didn't look in his direction, but I couldn't help but wonder why he was here. He didn't usually come out to these events. Almost never.

"They're clearly together, if you're wondering. This is good, right?" Rosie prompted at my shoulder.

I looked at her and shook my head, feeling a little sick inside. "Maybe it's good for me, but I know what that means for her."

A panicky feeling spiraled through me, swamping me with mixed emotions. Maybe if Rich got serious with someone else, he would leave me alone because he would have someone else to treat like shit. I felt so absolutely horrible for thinking that. I took a slow breath, trying to ignore the churning sick feeling inside.

Fiona appeared, sliding her hand through my elbow and squeezing. Within a minute, my friends encircled me. I knew why they were doing this. Although I had never gone into detail about everything that went down with Rich because it was too embarrassing, and I was so deeply ashamed, they all knew he had been abusive to me, and they were so protective. I loved them for it. Rosie stayed on one side, Fiona on the other, and Haven and Quinn appeared across from me.

I felt safe with my friends. They couldn't completely distract me from Rich. His presence was like a black cloud in my psyche if he was nearby. I didn't know if I would ever get to a point where he could be neutral for me.

Fiona leaned over at one point. "They're leaving."

"Thank you," I whispered under my breath.

Fiona was newer to Fireweed Harbor, but she'd quickly become a good friend. She was quiet, strong, and deeply loyal. A few minutes later, Fiona squeezed my elbow. "He's out the door."

Wyatt and Griffin, the other set of Cannon twins, joined us. I was briefly distracted when I noticed Wyatt's eyes lingering on Rosie. He was seriously checking her out. I surreptitiously slid my gaze toward Rosie to see her cheeks were pink. She stole a look at him before staring down at the glass in her hand. The moment passed after Wyatt looked away when Griffin said something to him.

I was still unsettled by Rich showing up

here and excused myself to go to the restroom. I needed a minute to gather myself. I threaded my way through the crowd, dipping into the back hallway. This was the area for the private offices, but I had permission to be back here. I'd actually worked at the restaurant when I was in high school. These days, when Haven and McKenna hosted events here, I sometimes helped with various miscellaneous tasks.

I'd turned into the break room just as I heard the hallway door open behind me. My nerves were on high alert. Whenever Rich was around, my nervous system took a while to calm down when he left. I was jumpy and edgy, and my fingertips tingled.

The quick footsteps caused anxiety to rise swiftly inside. Just when I glanced around to find somewhere to hide, I heard, "Tessa."

Adam's voice rang like a bell inside me. Although my nerves were stripped raw, I instantly felt soothed. I turned to see him standing in the doorway. Whatever he saw in my eyes, he moved quickly toward me, stopping immediately in front of me. "Are you okay?"

It felt as if my emotions were against my skin, and I couldn't contain them. Despite the shock and almost bewilderment at what was happening with Adam, I felt completely safe with him. I opened my mouth to tell him I was fine, but instead, a sob slipped out.

He murmured something before folding me in his arms. I cried with my face buried in his chest. I didn't feel like I had to explain anything. He simply held me. His embrace was strong and sure. The emotional storm passed, abating as quickly as it had rushed in. I took a shaky breath and finally lifted my head.

Adam smoothed my hair away from my face with one hand. "Are you okay?"

"Yes."

I had no idea how he knew, but he knew I needed a minute. "I'll wait here." He held the bathroom door open for me. A moment later, I stood in front of the mirror and stared at my reflection. My mascara was smeared on my cheeks, my nose was running, and my eyes were puffy.

I quickly splashed water on my face and wiped the mascara off my cheeks. I ran hot water over my hands to warm me and get rid of the cold, tingly feeling. On the heels of another deep breath, I dried my hands and stepped out of the bathroom.

Adam was leaning against the wall beside the door.

"Thank you," I said.

His eyes held mine. "I'm here whenever you need me."

He walked me out to my car where it was parked across the street behind Fireweed headquarters. Once I was in the car and buckled in, he rested his hand on the inside edge of my door. "When can I see you again?"

Chapter Twenty-Four

ADAM

One month later

Tessa: *Please.*

My lips curled as I read her one-word reply to my question about whether I could stop by tonight.

I was deeply in love with Tessa and wanted to see her every night. As it was, I saw her almost every night. On the nights Eric was with his father, I spent those entirely with her. Usually, she came to my place.

I hadn't spoken of love since the time I told her I thought I was falling in love with her. But I knew I loved her. Kenan had taken to teasing me about it on the regular.

Case in point, he came walking into my office at that moment.

"How's Mr. In Love?" he asked when he plunked down in the chair across from my desk.

A chuckle rustled in my throat. "You sound pretty confident about that," I quipped.

He considered me for a few beats, his smile fading. "I am. The more important question is, are you?"

My heart gave a hard thump, almost as if to answer. "I am."

"So what are you gonna do about it?"

I let out a short sigh. "Isn't that the kicker? I'm not sure how Tessa feels, and I don't know what to do about Rich. She's afraid if he knows we're involved that he'll make things hell for Eric. For obvious reasons, I don't want that."

"Of course not," Kenan returned. "Maybe you should talk to Colin."

I leaned back in my chair, rocking a pen between my fingers. "I don't think Tessa would appreciate that. I don't think she would mind me asking him something, but I don't want to be overbearing and act like I know what's best."

"Here's an idea: tell her you love her, tell

her you want this to be a real deal, and walk through that fire together."

I looked at him for a long moment before a wondering laugh followed. "You make a good point. That's probably what I should do."

"It *is* what you should do. I'm not saying Rich can't make her life hell. But Colin is a damn good attorney. If shit goes sideways, the town loves you. Every now and then, it's good to be a member of the Cannon family."

Before I could reply, he added, "And people like us even more because fucked-up shit *has* happened in our family, so they don't think we have it easy. Plus, you're everybody's favorite."

"What the hell are you talking about?"

My brother shrugged. "There's me—"

"And me," Blake called as he walked into my office, followed by Rhys.

"What's happening? Family meeting?" I asked.

"Well, we're missing McKenna, Wyatt, and Griffin, so no," Rhys teased.

"What are we talking about?" Blake asked, gesturing between Kenan and me.

"Tessa." That was Kenan's one-word response.

"Oh wait, are you finally going to admit you're seeing Tessa?" Blake asked.

My eyes narrowed at Kenan.

He held his hands up. "Dude, I haven't said anything to anybody. I'm a vault." He tapped two fingers on his temple.

Blake rolled his eyes while Rhys cast me a knowing grin. "Dude, I drive past your house on the way home. I've seen Tessa's car there a few times."

"Do you think McKenna knows?" I couldn't help but ask.

"Course she does," Blake piped up. "She and I were going to bet on when you two might fess up."

I let out a laugh on the heels of a sigh. "So what were you talking about when you said, 'there's me'?"

"Just that you're everybody's favorite in town," Kenan explained.

My brothers nodded in unison. "What?" I sputtered.

"Yeah, I'm the oldest, so people have opinions about everything I do," Rhys chimed in. "And they are the two jokers." Rhys gestured back and forth between Kenan and Blake.

"People like us, but you're the steady, quiet guy," Blake offered. "You give off the good-guy vibe like you're there for anyone. And you are."

"It's genuine," Kenan added.

Bemused, I shrugged.

"What's this all about anyway?' Rhys asked.

"I told Adam he needs to tell Tessa he loves her and be there with her through whatever bullshit her ex tries to pull," Kenan said flatly.

"Damn straight," Blake chimed in.

"The whole family has your back," Rhys added.

My heart felt squeezed tight. Sometimes it drove me nuts to have a big family, but we had been through some shit together, and we took care of each other.

"Thanks," I said simply.

"Do we have to keep pretending we don't know about you and Tessa?" Blake asked.

I rolled my eyes. "Not with me. But let me talk to Tessa. She's pretty stressed about how Rich might react. Not for herself, but for Eric."

"Rich is a fucking asshole," Rhys pointed out.

"No shit," I agreed.

Chapter Twenty-Five

ADAM

That night, I parked in the out-of-view spot behind Tessa's house and lightly knocked on her kitchen door.

Seconds later, she opened the door, and my lips curled into a smile. Her hair was up in a messy ponytail, and she wore one of my sweatshirts. It shouldn't matter, but I loved it when she wore something of mine.

"Hey," she whispered, opening the door a little wider.

I slipped inside, and she closed the door quietly behind us before catching my hand in hers. We tiptoed into her bedroom. As soon as the door clicked shut, I caged her between my arms and kissed her.

She tasted a little sweet and smelled like

sugar. When I lifted my head, I felt breathless at the rush of emotion.

"How was your day?" I managed to ask.

She smiled. "Good. They're switching me to the earlier weather report, which will be great so I don't have to juggle finding babysitters."

"Nice. I know that'll work better for you and Eric." I stepped back, reaching around her to make sure the door was locked.

We'd been lucky so far. Not once had Eric walked in on us, but we were both sensitive to that possibility.

I toed my shoes off by the door and caught her hand in mine. I took a few steps back before I sat on the foot of her bed. She stood between my knees. "Can I say something?"

Her eyes held mine as she nodded. "Of course. What is it?"

I actually felt a little nervous, but I knew my brothers were right. Either Tessa and I treaded water and stayed in limbo with our relationship or I tried something else. I would hand her my heart and see what we could do together.

I held her hands in mine and looked up in her eyes. "I love you, Tessa. And I'll wait for you. I'll wait until you're ready. I want you to know that I'm here, and I'm ready whenever you are. I am *not* saying this to rush you. I just want you to know how I feel."

She blinked, and a tear rolled down her cheek. I lifted my thumb, swiping it away. "What is it?"

"I love you too. But..." She let out a shuddery breath.

"I know you're worried about Rich, and I completely understand. I'm here, and we'll deal with it together. I know you don't want money, but I have plenty of it. When it comes to lawyers, that's kind of handy," I pointed out.

Tessa's lips twisted to the side. "I know." She paused for a few beats before asking, "What do you want?"

"You. Us. Every day. I want you not to be afraid. What do you want?"

"All of that." She paused again, chewing on the inside of her cheek. "Since Rich started seeing someone else, it's been better."

"Maybe we stop sneaking around and see how it goes. Let me at least get you an alarm system. Then you don't have to be worried about him showing up here."

Tessa never spoke of it, but I knew she worried about it. Whenever I left her house, she would peer out the windows and check on things. Witnessing her anxiety created a literal ache in my heart.

She held my gaze for a few beats before she nodded. "Okay, let's do it."

"Do what? I really didn't tell you this to pressure you. I just wanted you to know how I felt. I thought maybe if I didn't tell you, we might end up in limbo forever."

She stepped a little closer, her palm landing on my cheek as her thumb traced along my cheekbone. "I love you, Adam. I don't want to be in limbo either. The only way through this is *through* it. Let me have you over for dinner with Eric soon. I know you know him, but that'll give me time to tell him that I'm seeing someone and you can come over. And it'll be like a regular thing."

"How do you want to handle it with Rich?"

"I'll ask Colin what I should do. If you want to come with me when I meet with Colin, that's fine with me. Deal?"

"Deal." My heart drummed hard and fast in my chest. I leaned forward, dropping a kiss in the sweet divot at the base of her throat.

Chapter Twenty-Six

TESSA

Rosie grinned over at me. "Things are looking good."

Fiona caught my eyes from where she sat beside Rosie and subtly arched a brow with a small smile teasing her lips.

"What do you mean?" I hedged.

Quinn snorted beside me. "You and Adam. I actually saw you together in public, and damn if you don't both look happy."

Haven was smiling as well, and I glanced around at my friends. "You think he's happy?" I couldn't help but ask.

"Oh my God. Are you serious?" Rosie rolled her eyes. "Adam is downright giddy when he's with you."

I couldn't help my smile. I almost giggled.

I was feeling downright giddy. Shockingly, Rich was minding his own business. Ever since he'd started dating, he finally seemed content to leave me in peace. Oh, I still had my moments when I woke during the night and fretted that I should probably warn his girlfriend. I didn't know how to go about doing that. I was just so relieved that he wasn't bothering me anymore. The nights he was scheduled to have Eric for visits were truncated to just dinner. He didn't even want to bother with more. Although part of me was sad that's how little he cared, the relief was far more powerful.

Little sprouts of hope were growing in the barren, burned patches of my heart. Whenever worries started getting noisy in my thoughts, I swatted them away. I desperately wanted it to be okay finally.

"Does Rich know you and Adam are seeing each other?" Haven asked.

"I think so. Obviously, I won't have a conversation with Rich about it. But this town is small. I don't see how he couldn't have heard. No matter what, at some point something had to give. I can't hide from Rich forever."

"Definitely not," Rosie said firmly. "I still think you're not telling us the whole story of how bad it was with him, and I totally understand. You don't have to tell us. You deserve to be treated well, and I'm really happy for you."

Quinn curled an arm around my shoulders, giving me a side hug. "Adam is a good guy."

Whenever I thought about Adam, the word that came to mind was safe. I felt *safe*. Beyond that there was the combustive force of our chemistry and the intimacy that was stitching us tighter and tighter together. But those only existed within the sense of safety I felt with him.

McKenna came walking in at that moment. We were having our casual get-together at Quinn's house tonight. "I'm late!" she announced as she shrugged out of her jacket and kicked off her boots by the door. She lifted three pizza boxes aloft. "I come bearing food."

"That makes up for everything," Haven teased as she reached for the plates in the middle of the table and began passing them around.

After we started eating, McKenna asked, "What did I miss?"

"We're all ecstatic that Tessa and Adam aren't hiding anymore," Fiona offered between bites of pizza.

"Let's toast to that." McKenna held up her glass of water, and we clicked our glasses together. Her eyes were warm as she smiled over at me a moment later. "That man is so into you. And I have to say I thought Adam was the least likely to fall."

"Really?" I couldn't help but ask.

"He's so serious. He was busy taking care of all of us when we were growing up, the classic middle brother. But then, when I think about it, it makes sense. He has a good heart. I think you two are good for each other."

Conversation moved along, and later that night, when Adam came over, I thought about McKenna's observation. I hoped we were good together. I just hoped somehow it would all hold.

———

"Hey, sweetheart." Adam's voice beside my ear sent a hot shiver through me.

He brushed a kiss on the side of my neck just below my ear, and goose bumps prickled over the surface of my skin.

"Hey." I felt the tug of my smile. The sense of joy rising inside was fizzy and bubbly, like champagne. That was my reaction to Adam all the time these days.

He reached for my hand, his grip warm as his fingers laced within mine. "Ready?" he asked.

"Always."

We fell into step beside each other. I was slowly getting used to doing things with Adam in public, as though we had a regular life. He was my boyfriend. We'd even done gone to two cooking classes together like we talked about. I'd scrambled up the courage to go here in Fireweed Harbor, and I'd loved it. All because Adam was with me.

I almost couldn't believe it. For years, I had assumed I would be stuck with Rich, because it seemed too risky to try to leave him. I had carried a weary sense of dread in my heart.

When I had somehow mustered the courage to actually leave, I had been so relieved. All I'd wanted was to be alone. The freedom of being free from the weight of Rich's abuse had been powerful.

I'd believed it would be disastrous for me to even try to date. And honestly, I hadn't thought I would ever be interested in a man again. Rich's jealousy had been so out of control. If I happened to look in the direction of a man, not looking at the man, but say because I was looking for a street sign, and a man happened to be standing near it, that led Rich to cold fury.

Ever since he had started dating, it felt different with him. Not that we interacted all that much. My interactions with him had been limited to court paperwork, drop-off times, or the occasional out-of-the-ordinary encounter in the community.

But when we met for drop-offs for Eric, it was like I didn't even exist to Rich anymore. He usually had his girlfriend with him. She would smile, and I would smile, and that would be it. I was still wrestling with the worry that I should say something to her about him, yet I had no idea how to go about handling that.

Being out in public holding a man's hand, a man who I actually liked, was far beyond what I had ever expected. Adam held the back door to the winery open, dropping my hand and coaxing me forward with his palm in the curve of my back. I savored every touch from him.

I took an unsteady breath. Anticipation mingled with a little anxiety spinning through me. I was pretty sure Rich had to know I was dating Adam, but I didn't know for sure.

"What do you think?" Fiona asked from where she stood by a round table in the corner of the employee break room.

Even though I had come and gone through here many times with permission from McKenna and the family, it felt different coming in here with Adam. It felt like I belonged.

My uncle David was seated at the table. He winked as he glanced over. "Hey, Tessa," he said as Adam and I approached.

"Hey, Uncle David. What are you doing working so late?" I teased.

My uncle was known for working late hours. He'd been the main chef here for years and years until he hired Fiona as the chef and stepped down to only administrative management. An array of plates was set out on the table.

"We're testing some new recipes," Fiona explained when Adam and I stopped beside her.

She gestured her hand in an arc over the table. "Please, try everything." She handed us a little notepad. Each plate had a number on it. "Just write the number and what you think."

"Can this be an official job?" I teased as I reached for what looked to be a scrumptious cheesy roll.

My uncle chuckled. "We could add a line item to the budget, but people are willing to taste test for free, so I don't think so."

Adam's hand fell away from my waist as he reached for a sample.

"What is this?" I wrote the number on my notepad as I held it up.

"It is a brie pastry with blackberries. I want to have some new specials for the holidays," Fiona replied.

"That's months away," I pointed out before I took a bite and moaned as the savory and tart flavors broke across my tongue.

She grinned. "It is months away, but we need time to plan."

I finished chewing and reached for the pencil. "Should I write moan-worthy?"

"You can write whatever you want," David replied.

"Were you part of the menu planning?" I asked him as I selected another item.

"I had input, but these are Fiona's ideas."

"Don't give me too much credit," Fiona said dryly. "Everything's derivative. There are so many recipes out there these days. I just try to come up with my own twist."

"This is absolutely delicious," Adam said after he finished chewing.

"Are you staying for locals' night?" I nudged my head in the direction of the restaurant down the hallway.

Fiona nodded. "I'll be out there in about half an hour."

My uncle stood from the table and rounded it to give me a quick hug. "It's good to see you." He glanced toward Adam. "You take good care of her."

Adam held his gaze. "Always."

My heart squeezed with a sharp, sweet pang when I felt Adam's eyes shift to me. I swallowed and took a breath. I wanted to fling my arms around him, but we were in public, so I had to keep myself together. Emotion tended to crest in startling waves when I was with him. I was trying to play it cool, to let this be a normal relationship. But I'd never had a normal relationship, if there was even such a thing. Rich was my only serious relationship. My view of relationships was distorted and damaged. When all was said and done, I felt lucky I had escaped.

My uncle squeezed my shoulder as he walked by. "Have a good night." He waved over his shoulder as he slipped out the back door.

A few other staff came into the break room. Word had traveled that there were samples to taste. With Adam's hand holding mine securely, we walked out to the restaurant and mingled with his family. The Cannon family could be a lot. I had been friends with McKenna since kindergarten, but with her being the youngest sibling, my interactions with her brothers had been mostly brief. Over the years of growing up with her, I'd listened to her various complaints of being teased and annoyed with different brothers. I'd witnessed the gaping silence about her family after their father had died.

It was nice to see the camaraderie they shared and how they had become closer in different ways now that they were adults.

Adam's mother stopped beside us at one point, smiling warmly over at me. "Hi there!"

"Hi. Nice to see you," I replied politely.

"I always love to see you, Tessa. I'm really happy to see you with Adam. I think you two might be perfect for each other," she said.

Adam was beside me, talking with Blake and Rhys about something. When I reflexively glanced his way, he gave me a reassuring smile. My cheeks felt heated when I looked back at his mother.

"Thank you," I said, unsure what else to say.

My bruised heart wanted to shout for joy and clap, to announce to the world that Adam and I were perfect for each other. But my anxiety knew better. I was deeply cautious and didn't dare hope for too much. I took a careful breath.

Adam happened to glance toward his mother at that moment. "What did you say to Tessa?" His tone was protective, as if he sensed my uncertainty.

His mother's eyes twinkled. "I told Tessa I think you two might be perfect for each other."

His gaze softened. "Might?" He squeezed my hand, and my heart flipped over in my chest.

McKenna and Jack came over to chat with us, and Fiona made her way out. Blake tugged her into a hug, giving her a lingering kiss. Nothing was too overboard about it, but whenever I saw them together, a tender intimacy almost seemed to shimmer around them. I loved that for her. I didn't like admitting it to myself, but a small part of me wished I could have something like that. I wouldn't quite call how I felt as jealous, but a pang of wishing for more than I thought I deserved.

Blake and Kenan were joking about something when I experienced a familiar and unsettling sense of awareness. The hairs rose on the back of my neck. Reflexively, I held still. I was relieved there was plenty of conversation flowing around me. I forced myself to wait several minutes before I carefully glanced around the room. Rich was here with his girlfriend. He wasn't looking in my direction at the moment, but I assumed he had been. It was all I could do not to run out of the room.

Adam squeezed my hand, and I glanced up at him. "Don't worry." His words were quiet, only for me to hear. "It's going to be fine. You're not doing this alone."

Tears stung my eyes, and my throat felt thick with emotion. At this moment, they weren't bad tears. They were tears of relief, of an immense gratitude. I had felt so alone for too long. It was almost surreal to realize I had someone standing right here with me, assuring me that I wasn't alone anymore.

Not much later, we left. We actually walked past Rich and his girlfriend. If Rich noticed us, he didn't give any indication. He had his arm around his girlfriend's shoulders, talking to someone I didn't recognize and gesturing toward the television above the bar.

My body hummed with a confusing muddle of emotions when we walked outside. But rising through the detritus of my fear and anxiety, so easily triggered by Rich, was a sense of triumph and a deep sense of love for Adam.

When he stopped beside his SUV to open the door for me, I placed my hand on his chest. He had his hand curled on the door handle. "What is it?"

"I love you," I said simply.

I didn't need him to tell me the same. I just needed to emphasize how much he meant, and how strong my feelings were.

He was silent before a wide smile unfurled across his face. "I'm a lucky man. I love you too."

He placed his hand over mine, where it rested on his heart. Joy rushed upward inside. It felt like cymbals clanging inside.

"I told you I would wait until you were ready."

Chapter Twenty-Seven

ADAM

I sifted my fingers through Tessa's hair, savoring the soft little sigh she made in her sleep. When I woke up with her, I experienced a sense of wonderment. Maybe I had experienced love before, but I'd been so young and definitely naive.

The love I had felt for Julie had been different. Now I could understand it was immature. After I had been so hopeful that I could prove that love would make me feel better about life and about the shitty hand I felt our family had been dealt.

I never expected I'd actually find Tessa and fall in love in this way. Our two flawed selves, the jagged pieces of our hearts hinged together and healed the slivers of bitterness left over. The losses in my life had made it possible for me to love Tessa the way I did.

Tessa shifted in her sleep, her knee bumping into the side of my thigh. She moved a lot when she was sleeping, often elbowing me or curling against me softly. Sometimes it was nice, and sometimes it was jarring. I loved all of it, all of her.

I sensed her coming awake, a subtle hum of electricity, of attention and alertness.

"Did I just stab you with my knee?" Her voice was a little raspy, and she cleared her throat when I chuckled.

"I was already awake."

She rolled closer to me. Because this was Tessa, and I was me, my cock was all, "Well, hello and good morning!"

Her warm skin was soft. I let my fingers slide through her hair to smooth my hand down her back and over the sweet curve of her bottom. I couldn't resist giving her a little squeeze.

She rose on an elbow, tracing lazy circles on my chest.

"How long have you been awake?" Her eyes twinkled with her smile.

"Not long."

Her palm slid down over my abdomen, and she gave my cock a bold teasing stroke.

"Good morning to you." She squeezed me as she grinned.

I couldn't resist angling my head to the side on the pillow and pressing lazy, open-mouthed kisses along the side of her neck.

"Good morning to you as well," I murmured between kisses as I teased my fingers between her thighs to find her hot, wet, and ready.

Her cheeks were flushed when I let my head fall back against the pillow again. "Do you think this will ever fade?" she asked.

"What do you mean?" I slid two fingers into her slippery wet core.

She bit her lip, letting out a little moan. "This, being crazy for each other." She stroked her curled palm around my length. I was hard to the point of pain and felt a little drop of cum roll out.

"Never," I bit out.

She dipped her head to bring her lips to mine, and we kissed lazily, a slow tangle of tongues. She shifted up, releasing her grip on my length and pressing her palm on my chest as she rose to straddle me. My cock was nestled in her slick folds when she rocked her hips slightly.

I let out a growl. Gripping her hips, I looked up at her. She was so fucking sexy—

her curls a tousle around her shoulders, her skin flushed from sleep, her eyes dark with passion. She stared down at me. Her hand was still on my chest, and my heart kicked against it, recognizing her touch.

"I love you, Adam."

My hands tightened, pressing into her skin. "I love you, sweetheart."

She reached between us as she lifted her hips. I felt her kiss against my crown a second before she sank over me, sheathing me in her rippling channel, the very heart of her.

———

Maybe an hour later, after we had showered and Tessa left with Eric, I made sure her place was locked up and headed into town. I parked at the office and walked the short distance to Spill the Beans Café. I had a long day ahead because we had monthly reports coming in, so I needed a kick-start.

When I walked in, Hazel was at the counter, moving the line along at a brisk pace as she handed coffee and baked goods to the customers. Her usual smile was wide when I reached the front of the line. She looked downright giddy. "What are you so cheerful about?" I asked.

"I am so happy about you and Tessa."

"This isn't new gossip," I teased lightly.

"It sort of is," Hazel said. "It's only been within the past few weeks that you two have actually been open. You have both been through your own challenges, and I think you deserve each other in the best possible way. Your usual?"

"Of course. Strong as you can make it."

She began prepping my coffee, adding, "You're going to get an extra shot of espresso. My eyes cross when I deal with numbers, and you do it all day."

I chuckled. "I appreciate it. I'll pay for that extra shot."

She waved dismissively. "Without your family's businesses in this town, things would be tight for us."

"Well, without Spill the Beans Café, I don't even know how Fireweed Industries would run since we relocated our headquarters back here."

Hazel grinned at that. When she took my money a moment later, her gaze sobered. "I *am* happy for you and Tessa, and I know Rich is seeing someone. He seems to be giving Tessa some peace now, but men like him don't usually change. Not when they're his age. I might've given him a little chance if he was younger because boys are stupid and reckless. Sometimes life has to give them a few hard lessons. Rich isn't young, and it was never impulsive with him. He's just mean but also charming and handsome." Her lips twisted to the side as anger flashed in her eyes. "Anyway, just don't let your guard down. I don't trust him."

"I think I can handle it, but I appreciate your concern," I said.

With my reply, scene upon scene, like those old slides on a projector, passed through my thoughts. My grandfather's face mottled red as he screamed at me about a chore not done well enough, him slapping Rhys hard across the face, and the sound of my oldest brother, Jake, crying in his bedroom at night. More than anything, those old memories elicited a familiar feeling—a sense of dread, exhaustion, and an awareness that was unique to having to always be on alert in the place where you were supposed to feel safe. Home.

"I know you can handle him," Hazel said. "Make sure to take care of Tessa and Eric."

Hazel's words echoed in my thoughts when I happened to see Rich at the gas station that afternoon. Rich pulled up after I was parked and already getting gas. He parked on the opposite side of the same gas pump. When I glanced over, not yet aware it was him, I simply nodded when our eyes met.

He spun his keys on his forefinger when he rounded the trash can between the sides of the gas pumps and stepped under the awning near me. "So you're seeing Tessa."

There was a hint of a question in his tone. "I am."

"I just wanted to say I'm glad. You have my blessing."

It wasn't his words, but the look in his eyes and the feeling he gave off, as though he were giving me permission.

I held his gaze. For a moment, it felt as if a challenge rose in the air between us. I knew Rich. I knew his kind, always jostling for dominance. I also knew how to ignore and defuse assholes like him.

As much as I wanted to tell the guy to fuck right off, I didn't. Even if he seemed to have backed off toward Tessa, they shared a son. For that reason alone, there needed to be peace. I simply nodded.

Just then, someone called Rich's name from inside the car where he'd left the door cracked open. "Have a good one," I said.

Moments later, I drove away. On the one hand, it was a nothing interaction. On the other hand, it rankled me that Rich felt the need to say anything.

In theory, I obviously believed two parents who weren't together should be on good terms. That was the best thing for any child they shared. But it was different with Rich. He didn't really give Tessa his blessing. With his words, I could feel his underlying sense of ownership of her.

Chapter Twenty-Eight

TESSA

As the weeks passed, I started to experience genuine happiness, something I'd questioned could ever be possible. My life was peaceful. I loved my job. Eric seemed to have accepted Adam easily into our world, and Rich was finally a neutral presence in my life. I would never forget how horribly things had gone with him, and I would never forget the way he treated me. But him ignoring me was a feeling beyond relief.

I often went to locals' night at Fireweed Winery before Adam and I started dating. Now, it was a weekly event because the Cannon family showed up in force.

I enjoyed going with Adam. I felt as if I was a part of something. McKenna had been one of my closest friends for years. During those years with Rich, I felt brutally alone, even when I was in crowds. It was so nice not to feel isolated anymore.

I squeezed Adam's hand lightly before tugging free. "I'm going to the restroom," I whispered. He gave me a quick kiss on the cheek, and heat tingled under the surface.

I loved being with him so much. I felt like a teenage girl sometimes—starry-eyed and in love. Yet there was a strength stitched into the fabric of our connection. We had both seen the dark side of others and how badly things could go. What we had together was precious.

Still smiling, I slipped into the restroom. When I stepped out of my stall a few moments later, Rich's girlfriend, Lisa, stood washing her hands at the row of sinks. Her eyes met mine in the mirror. That worry in the back of my thoughts scurried forward. I didn't know how to have the conversation I wanted to have with her. The damage Rich had done was so deep I sometimes wondered if it was me, if *I* was the reason he had been abusive and controlling.

I tried to look anywhere but at her, as I glanced down at the sinks. As my eyes bounced around, they landed on some bruise marks on the inside of her forearm. I could see it in the mirror. I knew what had happened. Fingertips pressed deeply into her skin with a force that hurt at the moment and left behind dark purple bruises. I recognized those bruises because I'd had them. More than once.

Abruptly, nausea welled in my throat, and my heart started pounding in a sick, dread-filled beat. I took an unsteady breath and swallowed as I lifted my eyes to hers. She was looking down at the counter. I presumed she was studiously trying not to pay attention to me, just as I would have when I was with Rich.

"Are you okay?" My words came out rougher and louder than I intended

Her eyes whipped up to meet mine in the mirror. I gestured to the bruises on her forearm when she turned off the water. She stared at me for several beats. I scrambled up my depleted courage.

"He left bruises on me just like that. He cracked one of my ribs once. I went to Juneau for the X-rays and lied about who I was at the hospital. He didn't hurt me much. It was the rest—the constant monitoring with the app on my phone, with the tag he put in my purse and on my car. If I can help you, I will. All you have to do is call me or text me. I'll come at any time. I got away, and I know you can too."

Her eyes were wide and bright with unshed tears as she stared at me. Her swallowing was loud in the room before she whispered, "Thank you." She started to turn away.

Reflexively, I reached for her, touching her lightly on the shoulder. Tears sprang to my eyes when she flinched. I stepped back, quickly dropping my hand. "I'm sorry, I didn't mean to scare you. Can I at least give you my number? I went to the shelter. That's what they told me to do. Save my number under somebody's name from work or something like that. You can call me whenever you need anything."

Her hesitation stretched. Just when I thought I'd made a huge mistake, she tapped her phone screen and handed it to me. I quickly typed in my contact, saving it under Joan when she told me to use that name.

———

Later that night, my body reverberated from little shocks of fear. From my therapist, I understood my system had been kicked into a trauma reaction—fight, flight, freeze, or fawn. She told me some people had a primary response, and others' reactions varied. Sometimes I wanted to fight. Sometimes I froze, and most of the time, I fawned. I'd done everything I could to smooth things over with Rich when we were together, to soothe him, to keep him from getting angry.

Eric was at the kitchen table doing his homework. "Mom, can you help me? I'm stuck."

"Maybe," I said, trying to keep the anxiety out of my voice.

"It's math." He sighed in frustration.

I reviewed the worksheet and the instructions. I knew the answer, but I remembered his teachers reminding me to help him get to the answer himself. This little math problem gave me something to focus on.

After walking him through to the solution, Eric grinned up at me. "Yay!"

I chuckled, lightly ruffling his hair. After Eric went to play his allotted time for video games, I wondered what time Adam might text me. He wasn't over every night, but more often than not. I was anxious about him coming over. I didn't know if I should tell him about my conversation with Rich's girlfriend. He knew I worried about her, and he'd reminded me time and again that I couldn't control the situation.

My phone rang, and I glanced down to see Rich calling. I didn't answer his calls, and I wasn't about to now. But he began calling over and over. Nausea was bitter in my throat as I tried to keep it at bay. After the fourth call, a text came through.

Rich: *You fucking bitch. If you ever talk to Lisa again, I will make you fucking regret it.*

My hands shook. I swallowed and took an unsteady breath before forcing myself to screenshot the text. I did that so he wouldn't know I read it. The full text showed on my screen.

My fingertips were numb and cold. I debated whether I should try to call Colin when another text from Rich came through.

Rich: *You better dump that fucker.*

I tried to take a deep breath, but I couldn't. That old, familiar sense of panic rose swiftly inside, causing black dots in my vision. I tried to breathe. I reminded myself frantically that this feeling would pass.

I had enough presence of mine to screenshot the second text. After that, I leaned over and put my head between my knees. I didn't know how much time had passed when I heard Eric's voice. "Are you okay, Mom?"

He sounded worried. I took an unsteady breath and straightened, trying to put something like a normal expression on my face. "I'm fine, honey."

"You only look like that when Dad says something scary." Eric stood in the archway between the kitchen and the hallway.

"I'm fine. I promise." That was a lie, but I needed to fake my way through this.

"I like it better when I just have to have dinner with Dad and don't have to stay the night. Can we keep it that way?"

I clawed up every ounce of composure I had and nodded. "I'll check with him."

I'd never promised Eric that I would leave his dad, but I promised him thousands of times in my heart.

He blinked. "Okay." He walked into the kitchen and put his small hands over mine where they were clasped together over my knees. "Things are better now. Just remember that. Adam is really nice."

I hugged him, holding on maybe too tight for a second. When Adam texted a little bit later, I lied and said I had a migraine.

Adam: *I can still come over.*

Me: *I really just want to rest.*

Adam: *Okay, text me in the morning.* 🤍 🤍 🤍

Chapter Twenty-Nine

TESSA

My thumbs hovered over my phone screen. I wanted to text Adam and break it off. I knew I had to—for Eric—but my heart hurt. It felt like Rich was once again pulling the strings of my life. I was nothing but a marionette he controlled from a distance.

I should've known better than to think he would accept me seeing anyone. Although part of me wished I hadn't said anything to Lisa, I hoped she was okay.

I wanted to take the coward's way out and just send Adam a text, but I owed him a face-to-face conversation. After I dropped Eric off at school, I called him.

"Hey, where are you?" I asked as soon as he answered.

"Still at home." His voice was warm, and a fresh sense of happiness spun in my chest.

"Can I stop by?"

"As if you have to ask," he teased lightly. "You're feeling better?"

"Uh-huh. I'm on my way. I just dropped Eric off at school."

"See you in a few."

My heart pounded unsteadily, and my chest felt tight as I drove to Adam's. I didn't want to do this, but I had to. I was running on adrenaline when I arrived and practically raced up his stairs.

Adam opened the door as if he'd been waiting for me. He was murmuring against my lips a moment later after he tugged me into the house. I let myself forget for just a moment why I was there and tumbled into our kiss.

By the time he lifted his head, I was breathless. He stepped back. "Would you like some coffee? Or should we go to Spill the Beans Café?"

My smile was shaky. "Coffee here would be great." I followed him into the kitchen, and he handed me a mug of plain black coffee. He knew how I liked my coffee. My heart twisted sharply because that tiny detail meant so much.

He turned, resting his hips against the counter and studying me. "What is it? You look worried."

I blinked. "How do you know I'm worried?"

"Because I know you."

I took a gulp of coffee, my hands curling around the mug and holding on as if it could somehow keep me from spinning out inside. On the heels of a deep breath, I blurted out, "I can't see you anymore."

Adam was quiet for a few beats. He set his mug down on the counter another moment later. "What did Rich do?"

"I screwed up. I saw his girlfriend in the bathroom the other night at the winery, and she had bruises on her arms. They were fingerprints. I know what those look like. I told her if she needed anything, I would help her. She must've said something to him. I don't know. He told me I fucked up. I know what that means. It'll come down to Eric again. It always does. He knows that hurts me the most. I can't risk that, Adam." Tears slid down my cheeks, and I kept holding that mug.

Adam pushed away from the counter, stopping in front of me. His hands rested on my shoulders, his touch strong and steady. I was cold inside and out, and I could feel the warmth radiating from his palms.

"We said we would do this together. I'm not going to let him do this to you or to Eric."

My lips were dry. He lifted a hand, gently brushing the tears off my cheeks with his thumb.

"I know we said that, but it's Eric. Eric is more important than us, than me. I need to talk to Colin and see what we can do. That's the only way maybe I can get—" I closed my eyes as I took a shaky breath before opening them again. "I don't want to do this. I love you." I swallowed through the ball of pain in my throat. "I have to try to make sure it's okay for Eric first."

"I understand. I do. We'll do what we were doing before and hide. I'm trying to respect what you're saying about Eric."

"Adam, you don't understand. Rich will do everything he can to control this. We can stay in touch. I'll text you every day. We can talk on the phone, but that's it. Not until I know it's going to be okay."

He reached for the mug I was clinging to and set it on the counter. He folded me into his arms and just held me. "Okay," he whispered into my hair. "Call me tonight. I love you."

When I left a few minutes later, after a desperate kiss, my tears were drying on my cheeks. The only part I didn't tell Adam was that I was lying about calling him. I couldn't bear it. I could handle texting, but that was it.

And I hated that I let him believe otherwise.

Chapter Thirty

ADAM

"Fuck," I muttered to myself before leaning back in my desk chair and spinning around to stare out the windows.

With our office in the heart of downtown Fireweed Harbor, I had a spectacular view. The sun was bright in the late afternoon, glinting like shards of glass on the ocean's surface. Boats bobbed in the picturesque harbor, and the mountains were verdant green on the lower flanks, with the jagged rocky peaks rising into a bright blue sky.

I'd loved this place since we moved back home even though home was filled with complicated, messy, and sometimes traumatic memories. I felt calmer here. Yet at this moment, I felt scattered inside with my thoughts jumping from one thing to the next. Trying to focus on numbers couldn't even soothe me.

I didn't have much of a temper. I suppose experiencing the abuse I'd watched and heard in my family, I'd unconsciously taught myself to be the opposite—quiet, slow to react in heated moments. At this moment, I wanted to find Rich and at least give him one hard fist to the face.

"Hey, what's wrong?"

My eyes landed on my twin brother when I spun in my chair. Kenan rested his shoulder inside the doorframe, his alert gaze holding mine.

"Oh, I forgot I left my office door open."

"Thrilled to see me?" His tone was dry as he pushed away from the door and walked into my office, closing the door behind him.

When he sat down in the chair across from my desk, I tipped my head to the side. "You could've asked if you could come in. I might be busy."

"You might, but it looks like you could use someone to talk to."

Kenan and I knew each other so well. My heart felt cracked sharp by pain as I looked at him.

"Tessa told me that Rich will create problems with Eric if she doesn't break it off with me." Tears stung in the back of my eyes, and I sucked in a breath through the mix of anger and pain tightening in my throat.

"Fuck that noise," Kenan said as he leaned forward in his chair. "There's only so much he can do. Quinn told me that ever since he's got his girlfriend or whatever—" Kenan paused, waving a hand dismissively in the air. "That he's not even having overnight visits. She thought that was a good thing."

I leaned back, running a hand through my hair. "Tessa ran into Lisa, the woman Rich has been seeing. She said she saw bruises on the inside of Lisa's arms, and she told her if she needed anything, she would help. Clearly, Rich found out. She'll win in court eventually, but Rich can make her life a living hell in the meantime. I just don't know what the fuck to do. I want to help her. I'll hire ten attorneys if I need to."

Kenan leaned forward and fetched a pen off my desk. He began to spin it between his fingers in a rhythmic motion. He'd always been a restless thinker. That was why he did his job so well. His official title was senior executive for Fireweed Industries, but he did anything and everything we needed. He hated doing the same thing day in and day out. It was a perfect fit.

"Talk to Colin," he finally said.

"I can try, but it's Tessa's call. I can't tell her what to do."

"Well, then talk to her about it. It doesn't make sense to me that he can threaten her like this."

"I know."

"If you need anything, we all have your back."

I held my brother's gaze as I nodded.

A little while after he had left, I pondered how much it meant to have a passel of siblings. When things were hard, even when they were messy and ugly, I knew our family was there. Maybe we didn't always get along, and hell, sometimes we drove each other insane, but we were a force to be reckoned with. It wasn't because of wealth. It was because we had a bond. Tessa must've felt so alone. She had her uncle here and her parents in Juneau, but that was it.

Although I had reservations, I texted her to ask about her attorney.

Me: *How are you? Thinking of you all day. Was wondering if you minded if I spoke with Colin. I want to get a sense of what he might recommend.*

Tessa: *I'm okay. About to head in for the evening weather report. I don't mind if you talk to Colin. It's nothing he doesn't know, but maybe it will help.*

Me: *I love you. We're going to get through this. I promise it will be okay.*

Tessa: *I love you too. I hope it will be ok, but I don't know.*

———

Colin steepled his fingers together as he leaned forward on his desk, nodding for me to continue.

"Rich is a fucking asshole."

"Tell me something I don't know," he replied.

"Tell me there's a way to stop this game he plays. He goes through their son to get to her."

Colin appeared much calmer than I felt. "I know. Welcome to family court."

I gritted my teeth. "I understand this kind of thing happens. I love Tessa. Obviously, I want to be with her. But this isn't even about me. I just want Tessa not to have to be afraid of this. I want her to be able to live her life in peace."

Colin tapped his fingertips together. "I

know. A new judge has been assigned to the case. There was supposed to be a hearing coming up, but it got rescheduled because of the retirement of the other judge. And, honestly, the delay is worth the wait. The last judge was local here and friends with Rich's parents. He should've recused himself, but he didn't."

"How is that even legal?"

Colin sighed. "There *are* ethics rules, but we have to decide when to file a complaint. In this case, he retired. Now, it means waiting another month for a hearing. In the meantime, make sure Tessa documents everything. It's best if she only communicates with Rich via text because that creates a record."

"There's nothing else we can do?" I pressed.

"Unless she wants to call the police and make a report."

At my resigned sigh, he nodded. "Even if it would eventually help, any legal involvement can ratchet up the situation."

Although Colin was gracious and wanted to help, I left a few minutes later, feeling helpless. I called Tessa, but I just got her voicemail.

———

Two weeks later

Tessa wasn't answering my calls. She was only texting. My heart hurt.

Chapter Thirty-One

TESSA

The weeks were passing. The job I loved was a challenge at the moment. I still loved it, but it was hard for me to focus. I missed Adam, and I felt trapped by Rich again. I kept telling myself it wasn't as bad as actually being with Rich. He was using Eric to keep me in line, to make sure I couldn't be happy.

"Just dinner?" Eric's voice punctured my train of thought.

I glanced sideways in the car where we waited to turn out of the pick-up line at school.

"Just dinner. I think."

"Dad never says until he decides to drop me off. It's so stupid," Eric muttered.

I opened my mouth to correct him, to

maybe say that he didn't need to call it stupid. But it *was* stupid, so I let it slide.

A few minutes later, I dropped him off with his dad. Lisa hadn't been with Rich the last time Eric and him had dinner, but Eric said they were still dating. I didn't know if I cared anymore. Of course, I wanted her to be safe, but it was out of my hands.

I left, still cold. It felt like I'd been cold ever since the night Rich sent me those texts. I went to work. The students had a new assignment to match distances in Alaska with distances in the Lower 48. It was fun, and our social media channels were busy with updates. It was one of the few things that could make me smile these days.

My phone vibrated with a text just as I parked behind the recording station. I pulled it out to see Adam's name on the screen. We were texting, and I knew he wanted me to call, but he actually respected that I just couldn't handle it right now. That made me love him all the more. Rich would've badgered me. Adam simply said he understood and he loved me.

Adam: *I'm missing you. I'll see you tonight on the weather report.*

Me: *If you decide to stay up late, I'm doing the*

early news and the late news. The guy who does the late report is out of town.

Adam: *I'll be watching both. Love you.*

Tears stung in my eyes.

Me: *Love you too.*

I *did* love him. And I didn't know what the hell to do about this mess. I truly felt like I was going to have to let go. I almost felt like I was dragging things out too much.

———

On the weather report

"Tonight will be crystal clear with possibly a show from the northern lights, our late summer ones. We have a question submitted from viewers about what causes the northern lights and the best times of year to look for them."

"Last, we will close with a viewer-submitted photo from the northern lights yesterday evening up in Barrow, Alaska. And now, back to Tara, who has the latest on the local news."

Once I knew for sure the camera had panned away, I unclipped my microphone and took a deep breath. As soon as I walked off stage, I glanced down at my phone screen. I was expecting to see a text from Rich asking me to pick up Eric after dinner.

There was no text. I told myself he would probably text later, immediately chiding myself for hoping for anything.

"How did it go?" I asked.

"Another great weather report," Tony, one of the tech guys, said as I walked past him.

"Thank you!" Tossing a smile his way, I walked into the room that passed for my office. It was a shared space with several desks and laptops.

I quickly tapped my keyboard to check my email.

"Hey." I glanced up to see Jerri Patson, who ran production for the evening news.

"Hey, what's up?"

She stepped into the room, closing the door behind her. *That* made me nervous. Jerri wasn't one to take time for a meeting in the middle of the evening news.

"Is everything okay?"

"I'm sure it'll be fine."

"Uh, okay?" I started to stand, but she gestured for me to stay seated. "Jerri, what's going on?" Anxiety rushed through me like a windstorm. I didn't know what was happening, but I knew it wasn't good.

"We received a message. Let me just play it for you. I don't know how else to explain it." She tapped her phone screen. "It came in through the station's main email. They forwarded the message to me."

Nausea rose swiftly, bitter and acidic in my throat. I stared at her phone where she set it on my desk. My heart was pounding so hard it hurt.

The message began to play. "Tell Tessa she won't see Eric again."

Cold blasted through me. My fingertips tingled, and my heart raced so fast I could hardly catch my breath. I blinked rapidly.

I had never spoken about what I'd gone through with Rich at work. I hadn't even told my friends until it was over.

"Look at me, Tessa." Jerri's tone was calm and clear. Her gaze was steady. "We've already called the police. You were in the middle of your broadcast when this message came in."

"Oh my God." I couldn't even cry. "Jerri, I'm really sorry—" I began.

She shook her head and reached a hand out, putting it over mine. Her touch was warm, contrasting with the freezing cold permeating every corner of my body.

"Obviously, you've not spoken about what happened before your divorce. I know something about what a messy divorce can be like. I went through my own when I left a man who abused me. We will do whatever we can to help you."

"How do we get my son back?" My voice cracked with the tears that felt cold as they rolled down my cheeks.

"The police are already here and tracing the message. Is there any reason to suspect that he would hurt your son?"

Swallowing was painful. "I don't think he would hurt Eric. Rich just wants to get to me. That's it. What should I do?"

It was a surreal feeling, but I had no idea what to do. I was frozen, inside and out.

"We'll do whatever the police recommend. While we wait, is there anyone you want to call?"

Wordlessly, I shook my head. There was a knock on the door. Jerri called for them to come in. It was Chelsea, one of the receptionists, with the police.

"I told them you were in here," Chelsea said, her concerned gaze landing on my face.

The following span of time was a blur for me. I was freezing through and through. The police were asking me questions. A few things stood out. When they called Colin with me and started reviewing my text messages, Colin explained that Rich's threatening was a pattern. I remembered them asking permission to call Eric's therapist, and her sharing how Rich thought therapy was stupid and how Eric had clearly stated repeatedly that he didn't even want to visit his father.

I remembered the phone call to Rich's parents where his mother was dismissive and said we were all overreacting, and the dead silence that fell in the room at her comments followed by the sound of her breath sucking in sharply when the police played Rich's message for her on speakerphone.

Finally, Colin and the police repeating to me that I needed to stay somewhere safe. They didn't want me to be alone. Everyone was concerned I was in danger from Rich. They asked me who could stay with me and the only person I could think of was Adam. With shaking hands, I texted him.

Me: *I need somewhere to stay tonight. Or someone to stay with me.*

Adam: *I'll be right over.*

Me: *I'm at work. Can you come here?*

Adam: *Of course. I'll be there in five minutes.*

"He says he'll be here in five minutes," I said to Jerri. Even my lips were tingling. I struggled to form words.

Jerri's warm eyes held mine. "Okay. We're all waiting here with you."

Colin sat in the chair in the corner at a round table. We had relocated to the conference room. "Will it be okay?" I looked toward him as if he could somehow answer. I could see the pained look in his eyes, yet he was calm.

"Just let the police handle this."

He didn't tell me it would be okay.

Chapter Thirty-Two

ADAM

I was running, probably too fast, down the steps at the offices just as Kenan was coming up.

"Are you okay?" he asked the minute our eyes met.

"Something happened. I'm going to meet Tessa at work."

"Should I come with you?"

Even though I had no idea what was going on, my gut knew it was bad. I didn't hesitate. "Yes."

Moments later, I almost caused a car accident by pulling out without looking.

"Ease up," Kenan said.

I took a breath and slid my gaze to his. "I will."

"Should I drive?"

"No." I didn't want to wait for us to switch seats.

"What the hell is going on?" he asked a moment later.

"All I know is Tessa texted me and said she needs someone to stay with her tonight. Considering that she dumped me because of Rich, I'm pretty sure something big is wrong. She didn't ask if I would stay. She said she needed someone to stay with her."

My brother nodded. Four minutes after I had received Tessa's text, I came to a jerking stop in the parking lot at the local news station. It was a satellite office for the broadcast station in Juneau and Anchorage.

"Have you been here before?" Kenan asked as we climbed out.

"Actually, no. I'm assuming we go in there." I gestured to a side door.

There were several police cars in the back, one of them leaving as we arrived, and a pair of officers coming out the side door.

I wanted to ask what was going on, but they were hustling. I was already feeling amped up higher.

"Fuck, I hope Tessa's okay," Kenan muttered under his breath.

"She texted me, so I'm assuming she's physically okay."

Jerri Patson, who I knew in passing and knew she worked here, was walking down the hallway. "Adam! There you are. Follow me."

A moment later, we were in a conference room. Colin Blackthorn was there, and two police officers along with Tessa. She was twisting a napkin in her hands.

As soon as she saw me, she leaped up. I rounded the table and pulled her into my arms. She was trembling and freezing cold. She buried her face against the curve of my neck, and I smoothed my hand over her curls. "It's okay," I whispered into her hair.

She kept trembling, and I could feel her trying not to cry, trying not to fall apart.

When she finally lifted her head, I still held her but loosened my arms slightly. "I don't know what happened, but it will be okay. I'll make it okay."

She blinked her tears away and sniffled. I lifted my hand, sliding my thumb across her cheekbone. She opened her mouth to say something but closed her eyes again and took a shuddering breath.

Tessa stepped back a little, and I reached for her hands to discover they were icy cold.

I glanced around, my eyes landing on Jerri, who had returned to the room. "Do you have something hot Tessa can drink, tea maybe?"

"Tessa, what happened?" I asked when Jerri turned to get something for Tessa to drink.

"I don't know what to do. The police said —" When she started speaking, it was as if the words alone were too much effort for her. She finally gestured over toward Colin where he was seated at the table, conferring with one of the police officers and Kenan.

Jerri reappeared with a cup of tea. "You need to sit down," she said to Tessa.

With Jerri guiding her on one side and me on the other, we got Tessa situated in a chair by the table. I sat on the other side. I glanced at Colin and the police officer. "Tell me what happened."

"This station received a message here on their main voicemail for Tessa. He has their son and is threatening to keep him if she doesn't come to him."

Tessa had her hands curled around the steaming mug of tea. I slid my gaze to her. She stared woodenly at the table. I sensed her almost locking herself away inside. I slid my hand up and down her back in a soothing pass, wishing I could impart some warmth to her, some calm. Yet I knew this was her biggest fear, that Rich would use Eric as a bargaining chip to get her back.

"So what's the plan?" I asked.

"We're working with the tech team and coordinating on the geo-location. The call came in from a cell. We should be able to locate him. In the meantime, we need someone to stay with her," one of the police officers explained.

"Tessa can stay with me," I said quickly.

"They said it's best if I go home because Rich might look for me there." Her eyes lifted to mine.

I didn't like that. At all. "Sweetheart, I don't want you in danger."

"I need to get Eric back."

I glanced at the two police officers seated near Colin. "Is it safe for her to go home if I'm with her?"

The police chief, Mike Taylor, looked at Tessa before meeting my eyes again. I knew Mike well as he was born and raised here like me, but he had also married Fiona's mother recently, so he was part of our extended family. "We think so. It would be ideal if it appears as if she's home alone. We will be parked nearby monitoring. She said she has security cameras on the front and the back of her house."

"She does." I glanced at Kenan.

"I'll stay with both of you," he offered.

"More is better, right?" I replied.

Tessa looked from me to Kenan to her attorney and to the police. "Just tell us what to do."

"If it appears you're home alone, Rich might come to your place. We want to limit who is at risk," one of the police officers cut in reluctantly.

"Oh, for fuck's sake. There's no way we're leaving her alone," Kenan said.

Mike looked between Kenan and me. "I know you all have a hard time staying out of things."

Kenan shrugged. "We take care of each other. I already texted Rhys," Kenan replied. "Wyatt wants to be there to help too."

Mike sighed. "You can't all drive over there. How are you going to do this in a low-key way? We've already done a sweep to make sure he hasn't hacked into any of her security cameras or put anything extra on her property. If he calls, keep him talking. What we want is an opportunity to negotiate."

I felt Tessa's tremble beside me and

turned my attention back to her. "What do you need?"

Her eyes lifted to mine, and the pain and fear flickering there cleaved my heart. "I just want Eric home and safe."

She looked over at Colin. "Please tell me after this that I'll finally get full custody."

"You will," Colin said simply.

I could feel the shudder in her breath. My heart ached, and emotions tangled inside. I felt relief that Tessa had called me, as well as fear and a raw anger toward Rich for playing these games with Eric and Tessa. They didn't deserve this. No one did. I felt an old sense of helplessness from childhood rising up underneath it all, back when I'd been too little to stop anything. I didn't want to hurt anyone; I never had. I just wanted those who did hurt others to fucking stop and for the truth to be out there about who they were.

"Adam." Kenan's voice broke through the emotional cacophony creating static in my thoughts. I looked over at him. "Wyatt and I will meet you there. We're gonna park over at Haven and Rhys's house. We can walk through the trees to where Tessa's place is."

I held his gaze and nodded. "I'll drive over with Tessa."

"No, you won't." Mike's voice cut through.

"Why not?"

"We want him to believe she's alone. You go with your brothers. All of you can walk through the trees. We'll check the area again to make sure he's not nearby before you do," Mike explained.

I gritted my teeth, but I knew Mike had a point. I leaned close to Tessa. "Are you okay to drive by yourself over there?"

"I don't know," she whispered.

At that moment, Rosie arrived in the doorway, hearing my question. "Maybe we leave Tessa's car here, and I drive over?"

Jerri chimed in. "Rosie called over here because they heard something on the scanner at the ER. I filled her in when Mike said it was okay."

Tessa glanced over. "Thank you, Jerri."

"I'll drop Tessa off," Rosie said firmly.

"That's a good plan." I caught Rosie's eyes, mouthing, "Thank you."

It physically hurt to part from Tessa in the waiting area a few minutes later. I placed my hands on her shoulders. "I love you. We're going to find Eric, and Rich won't get away with this."

Tessa's cheeks were pale, and her eyes red. "Okay."

"I'll see you in about a half an hour. I love you," I repeated.

Chapter Thirty-Three

TESSA

"It's going to be okay," Rosie said, her tone firm as if she could will her assertion into fact.

"What if it isn't?" The fear and anxiety spinning like a whirling dervish through me kept my doubts in play.

My friend looked at me. "Okay, what I'm about to say is going to sound really fucked up," she warned me.

"Um, okay?" I let out a ragged sigh.

"Rich wants you. He doesn't want Eric. I know Rich is an asshole, and I'm still confident you haven't told us just how bad things were. You don't have to. I completely understand." I swallowed, the knot in my throat beyond the point of aching too sharp. "I don't believe Rich would hurt Eric. Oh, he'll pull some kind of bullshit like this. But I don't believe he would hurt Eric. I just don't. I might turn out to be wrong. But ask yourself, would he hurt his own son?'

I contemplated her question. She had a point. I honestly didn't think Rich would hurt Eric. Oh, he would be dismissive, he would be a jerk, and more than half the time, he couldn't be bothered to deal with his son. But what he wanted was to make my life hell. I'd known when I was leaving him that I was violating something that meant more than I could even imagine to him. I'd injured his pride deeply. My mistake in offering to help his girlfriend was not realizing that would remind him of what he had lost. That I had the strength to see him for who he was and walk away.

Rosie came to a stop sign and glanced over. I met her concerned gaze. "I think you're right. I don't think he would hurt Eric."

She nodded, just once. "You are a strong woman, one of the strongest I know. You can, and you will get through this. I'm going to drop you off, and those overprotective Cannon brothers will come to your house and make sure you're safe. We will find Eric, and it *will* be okay."

While I didn't feel her confidence, I appreciated it. "Okay," I whispered.

In short order, Rosie dropped me off at home, making a show of talking to me when the car door was open as I climbed out. "I can give you a ride in tomorrow if you need it."

I felt vulnerable and exposed as I jogged from her car to the house and let myself in. My hands shook as I locked the door. I had no idea how long it would be before Adam and his brothers might get here. I knew they planned to walk through the trees from the street where Rhys and Haven lived and come to my kitchen door because it wasn't visible from the front.

I was shivering cold, and my fingertips tingled again. I didn't know what to do. I sat down at the kitchen table and placed my phone on it. I checked again to make sure the volume was on. Then I stared at it.

I nearly jumped out of my skin when it chimed loudly as a text came through. As I slid it closer, my heart pounded. It was a text from Rich. I couldn't even remember what I was supposed to do.

Just when I started to panic, there was a

light knock on my side door, and I glanced up to see Adam. I hurried over and opened the door. He walked in and carefully closed the door behind him.

"Rich texted. I haven't read it, and I can't remember what to do." I could hear the panic in my own voice.

"We're supposed to read it. Let's just see what it says," Adam said, his tone level.

"You read it. Please," I whispered. My lips were numb.

Adam quickly spun the phone around before holding it up to my face so that it opened.

My pulse raced in a stumbling, sickening beat. My throat burned from the acid of the bile rising. My stomach was a churning mess. "What does it say?"

Adam scanned it, his eyes narrowing and darkening with anger before he lifted his gaze to mine. "He'll trade Eric for you."

"Okay. Where do I meet him?"

"Tessa, are you insane?"

"No. I'm terrified, and I want to know that my son is safe."

Adam closed his eyes, his jaw clenching tightly. One of his palms was flat on the table, and I watched as it curled into a tight fist. He forcibly stretched it open. When his eyes met mine again, his shoulders rose with a deep breath. Just then, there was a tap on the door.

I leaped up, hurrying across to see Kenan and Wyatt when I peered through the side window.

Adam was on my heels. "Tessa! You're supposed to let me let them in. It could've been Rich."

I spun around. "I don't care!" I felt jumpy inside with restless, unsettled energy coursing through me.

Adam reached around me to open the door and let his brothers in.

Although I was still terrified for my son, and it literally felt as if my heart had been ripped out of my chest, a strange sense of calm fell over me. It felt sort of like a curtain surrounding me. I wasn't delusional. I knew exactly what was happening. It was just that the worst had almost happened, and now I was solely focused. I wasn't worried about myself. I just wanted Eric to be okay.

I distantly heard Adam talking, and my awareness clicked into place again as I turned to listen. He flung a hand in the air. "Rich wants to trade Eric for her, and Tessa thinks that's a good idea." Adam spun away from his brothers and began pacing.

Kenan focused on Adam while Wyatt shifted his attention to me. He took several steps and stopped in front of me. "How are you doing?" His tone was calm, and I needed that calmness.

"Well, I'm not okay at all. But I don't think Adam understands," I explained.

"Maybe, maybe not. We're calling the police to let them know. We'll do whatever they recommend," Wyatt said. He placed a palm on my shoulder, his touch strong and soothing as he squeezed before his hand fell away. He was already lifting his phone and calling the police on speaker.

"Chief Mike Taylor."

"Rich texted Tessa. Wants to trade her for Eric. Adam is understandably upset. What should we do?" Wyatt asked without preamble.

Whatever Kenan had said to Adam, he appeared to have calmed considerably. He and Kenan came to stand on either side of me. Adam curled an arm around my waist, holding me close to him. Even though I could sense his unrest, I felt comforted. Because it was Adam, and I knew he loved me.

"You're not going to like my suggestion," Mike said on the phone.

I slid a look at Adam as he closed his

eyes. I felt the deep breath that he took. "You're gonna say Tessa should do this."

"Yes, but we have a plan. Rich is desperate. Whenever people do things like this, they are desperate. He may seem calm, but he's not. I know Rich," Mike said. "You guys know him too, and Tessa knows him better than any of us. He's always had a reputation for flying off the handle. He's not a cool, calm, collected kind of guy. He always lets his temper get the best of him. At the moment, he might think he has it under control, but he doesn't because he's done something stupid. Tessa, we need you to share your phone like we talked about so I can see what's happening on your phone."

The next few minutes passed swiftly. Adam was considerably calmer because he had something to focus on, the logistic steps needed to connect the police to my cell.

Mike basically told me what to say but had me text it how I would say it.

Me: *You know I'll do anything for Eric. Just tell me where to meet you. Who is meeting us there to pick up Eric?*

I had called my parents in Juneau at some point this afternoon. Even though they wanted to fly here, they were waiting until the police updated them. I knew they would meet Rich, but my first choice was my uncle David. He would be the least reactive in the situation, and Rich actually liked him.

"Why can't I go?" Adam asked while we waited for Rich's reply to my text.

The police chief was still on Wyatt's speaker. He interjected, "Because you can't keep your cool either. I trust you far more than I trust Rich and I don't think you'll do anything dangerous. You've had a lifetime of controlling your temper, but Rich won't go for it. We need someone neutral. Let's see what Rich says. If he suggests someone, we might go with that."

Rich's reply came as Mike finished speaking.

Rich: *I'll see you in an hour at the Lupine trail. My mom can pick up Eric.*

I clenched my teeth. Rich's mom and I had never gotten along. "She's been pissed off at me ever since I left," I muttered.

"That's fine. I can deal with Barb," Mike said.

I took a slow breath. Of all the things I was in a sheer panic about, my mistrust of Rich's mother shouldn't get to me. But it did. Because I knew she knew. She knew how he treated me, and she didn't care.

Adam's palm circled between my shoulder

blades. I savored the contact and bit back the urge to argue with the police chief.

"Are you sure?" I asked.

"I've known Barb for years. She's married to a man who's a lot like her son. I can understand why you don't trust her, but she'll do what's right for Eric," Mike said.

Even if I didn't want her involved, I knew he was right on that count.

"Okay. What do we do now?"

Chapter Thirty-Four

ADAM

I sat beside Wyatt on a fallen down tree. "I can't fucking believe this," I muttered.

Wyatt slung his arm around my shoulders, his touch strong and solid. "Mike knows what he's doing. Griffin and Kenan are right over there, and Rhys and Blake are on the other end of the only way out for Rich. That's not even counting the police."

"I love Tessa and Eric," I said simply, my chest aching.

"Of course you do. One way or another, it'll be okay."

I took a slow breath. "I hate men like Rich."

"Yeah. And we know men like him, including our grandfather who's sitting in prison." Wyatt's tone was dry and almost matter-of-fact.

I paused internally for a moment and tried to call up that old anger—my childhood twisted, confused, and helpless anger. All I felt was a void.

"I'm pretty sure Rich will be in prison soon too," Wyatt added.

My mind skipped back about a half an hour.

"Tessa, I love you," I'd whispered in her ear. I'd brushed her tangled curls away from her face. I hadn't wanted to let her go. At that moment, she had more strength than I did.

I took a shaky breath. She'd left with the police chief.

"How much longer do you think it'll be?" I asked.

Wyatt glanced at his watch. "Ten minutes, give or take."

I was having trouble focusing. I kept trying to picture Tessa's eyes, the wisdom and courage held there.

Her love for her son was carrying her through this. I was feeling selfish. I wanted them both.

The wait felt endless. Out of the quiet came a loud shot. I recognized Rich's voice. I leaped to my feet, every muscle ready to move.

Within a second, I ran through the forest with Wyatt hot on my heels.

Rich was at a distance waving a gun. I didn't see Tessa at first. Adrenaline was pouring through me. My body felt nearly electrified as I looked around for her. I kept my gaze locked on Rich once I circled back around.

Just then, he raised his hand, and another loud shot rang out. Rich spun. There was a blur of motion, and Rhys was suddenly beside him. After a quick tussle, he snatched Rich's gun and immediately emptied the bullets into the dirt.

Rich swore up a storm. I still didn't know where Tessa was until I heard her voice. My heart literally felt like it might crack my ribs as it flew upward in my chest and lodged high in my throat.

My gaze circled until I saw her. I bolted to her side, ignoring the commotion of the police, Rich, and my brothers.

"Tessa!" I reached her, stopping beside her and instantly checking her over.

"I don't know where Eric is." Her voice was trembling.

"Here!" a voice I didn't recognize cried out.

Spinning again, I searched out the voice to see a woman I vaguely knew, Barb, Rich's mother. Eric was beside her, holding tight to her hand.

Tessa cried out and ran for Eric. She fell to her knees and folded him in her arms. I followed closely but gave her space. I knew she needed this moment. "Mom. I'm okay," Eric insisted.

She rocked back on her heels and ran her hands down his cheeks before they landed on his shoulders. "Sweetie, I'm sorry."

"Mom, it's not your fault. Dad's a jerk. I didn't even know what he'd really done until we drove out here," Eric explained.

Tessa clapped a hand against her chest, balling it tightly into a fist.

"Do you need a minute?" I asked.

Eric was starting to look scared as he stared up at his mom. She couldn't even speak. "Hug her," Eric ordered me.

I could definitely do that. I wrapped Tessa in my arms and held her as she shook.

Gradually, her trembling slowed. I glanced over her shoulder to see Rich's mother comforting Eric. Obviously, I didn't know Eric the way Tessa did, but he seemed remarkably okay. Considering he'd just shared that he didn't realize what was happening until moments before this, I suppose that helped him.

"Eric's safe," I murmured into Tessa's hair.

Her shoulders shuddered with her ragged breaths. One of her arms was banded tightly around my waist, with her other palm pressed flat against my chest. After a few more moments passed, she lifted her face to peer up at me. The look in her eyes nearly broke me. A combination of deep sadness mingling with fear and intense relief flickered through her gaze.

"Eric's safe," I repeated.

She glanced around, her eyes tracking to Eric immediately. He was gesturing wildly with his hands. Kenan and Rhys had walked over.

"He's safe, and so are you," I said.

She blinked and brought her eyes back to mine.

"I love you." Those three simple words were my promise. "Now, go to him."

I could feel her trying to gather herself together as she turned. She reached for my hand. I knew I needed to let her lead this, but I was heartened that she reached for me.

She could handle all of this herself, but I wanted to be there for her, to be there for them.

When we reached him again, Eric looked up. "I'm fine, Mom."

Still holding tight to my hand, she reached down to smooth her other hand over his hair. "I can see that. Tell me what you need. A hug?"

He blinked up at her, and I could see the tears shining in his eyes. With a soft sound in her throat, she released my hand and lifted him into her arms. She held on tight, telling him over and over that she loved him and he was okay.

The police had already gotten Rich out of sight, which was the best for Eric and Tessa. Eric finally lifted his head from her shoulder. She kissed him quickly on his cheek as he smiled at her. The storm of tears had already passed for him. I knew from my childhood that the trauma of moments like this could subside quickly.

The scars Rich had inflicted on Tessa and Eric would always be there, but they would heal. With the police handling the situation, the next span of time passed in a blur. They were placing Rich under arrest. Mike assured

Tessa that they would argue against him being let out on bail.

When I looked at Tessa's face a while later, the release of tension she'd been carrying for years at this point was evident. She looked exhausted, but the tight anxiety had faded from her eyes.

After checking in with my brothers and hugging all of them, I turned to search out Tessa again. I realized, with the momentum of the urgency ever since she had called me earlier, I didn't know if she wanted me to be with her and Eric tonight.

She was stepping back from a hug with McKenna, who'd somehow materialized here in the midst of all of this. My sister met my eyes. "You take care of her."

"As if there's any question of that," I said softly. Glancing at Tessa, I held her eyes. "Always."

"Do you want me to stay with you tonight?" I asked her a moment later.

We were still surrounded by others, but Wyatt, Griffin, and Kenan had gotten Eric occupied with a game of trying to hit a mark on a boulder with a rock. While it seemed maybe out of tune with the past few hours, I knew Eric needed to focus on something other than the intensity and fear of these moments.

Chapter Thirty-Five

TESSA

Do you want me to stay with you tonight?

As if the answer was anything other than always.

Adam's eyes glinted in the dusk. Even though I knew he had moments in the past few hours when he wanted to tell me what to do, to take control of the situation, he hadn't.

I reached for his hand.

"I told you I'd wait for you," he said, his tone low and clear.

My heart felt as if it might burst out of my chest. The rhythm of its beat was strong and steady, and joy mingled with the intense relief I felt at Eric being safe.

"If it's not a good time because of Eric—" Adam began.

I placed a finger over his lips. "I want to stay with you tonight." I glanced over at Eric, who was smiling when Kenan threw a rock at another rock. It didn't take much to lighten a stressful moment. Kids were so resilient.

I was profoundly grateful to Adam's family for being here and for being the distraction my son needed after the moments of fear he must've experienced when he realized what was happening.

Bemused, I shook my head as I glanced over at Adam. "What are they doing?"

His lips curled at the corners as he rolled his eyes. "If there's nothing else to do, you can always throw a rock at a boulder. As far as I can tell, they're all trying to see who can most accurately hit that mark. Fun stuff."

Joy fizzed inside me, and I burst out laughing. A part of me couldn't believe I could even laugh. But I was simply emotionally overwhelmed, and laughter was a deeply needed release valve.

I didn't know when I would have time to process all of this or how long it would take. Right now, I was relieved my son was safe and Adam was here. Really, that was all that mattered.

"Your place or mine?" Adam asked.

"I'd say yours, but I think it's best for Eric to be in his own room tonight."

———

Hours later, the adrenaline had dissipated from my system. Before we left to come home, I'd had a moment with Rich's mother. I wouldn't say that I would ever feel totally comfortable with her, but I trusted her in a way I didn't think was possible. When it mattered, when it really *really* mattered, she had done the right thing.

Barb had also apologized to me. When she walked away, I realized she was going home to a man who probably treated her like Rich treated me, and it broke my heart. There was only so much I could do. The police chief had put his hand on my shoulder when I'd reflexively moved to follow her as if I could fix it.

"She knows her options. Maybe you staying in touch with her and seeing what happened with her son and grandson will help her take the steps she needs to," he said gently.

I hated that I felt peace for the first time in years. Honestly, since the very first time Rich had yelled at me.

I took an unsteady breath and let it out. I had tried to talk some with Eric, but when we got home, he just wanted to play a video game and relax. I knew there would be more to process later, but he had a therapist, he had me, and he had Adam. We would process when the time was right.

I looked up at Adam. My hips rested against the kitchen counter with Adam's hands curled around the edge.

"Let's go to bed," I said.

His smile was slow, and my belly spun in flips.

With his hand warm around mine, I led him into the bedroom. In the year and a half I had been here, this tiny apartment had felt so cozy and safe. Yet, finally tonight, the thread of tension pulled taut inside as a result of Rich's mere presence in our world had snapped free. With Adam here, the degree of safety and comfort I felt was beyond anything I could've imagined.

A moment later, the door closed with a soft click behind us. Adam was right behind me, his hand still holding mine. The burgeoning need for him felt like a fire kindling inside, the flames rising higher and higher between us.

"Tell me something, Tessa."

"Anything," I whispered.

He paused, considering his words. "I love you. I can't imagine my life without you. These past few weeks have been really difficult. I'll still wait until you're ready, but how do you feel about us now?"

Chapter Thirty-Six

ADAM

I meant what I said. I would wait until Tessa was ready for a commitment. But the emotions I felt for her ran deep. I wanted a life together.

She didn't even blink. I barely took another breath before she replied, "I love you. You don't have to wait. I want us. I want this life with you. We'll figure out the details. I'm never going to let Rich get in the way of us again."

She closed her eyes, her shoulders shaking as she took a breath. She released my hand and placed her palm over my heart when she stepped closer. "I need you. Now."

She leaned up as I dipped my head. Our lips met in a fierce, devouring kiss. We broke apart only because of the desperate need for oxygen.

Her palm slid down my chest in a bold stroke over my swelling arousal. I meant to take control of the moment, but Tessa snatched it right out of my hands. There was a wildness to her, an intensity I hadn't experienced before. Beyond being apart for too many weeks, the unsettling events of tonight were streaks of lightning in a dark sky, illuminating everything at this moment.

She yanked at the buttons on my fly, swiftly kneeling. At the last second, with her palm curled around my swollen length, her eyes angled up to mine. "Is this okay?"

As if it were anything but. "Please," I rasped.

I felt the kiss of her lips before she drew me into her mouth with deep suction. I breathed deep, clinging to my control as my fingers laced into her hair. My release was already threatening. Maybe another time I would've just let it go, but I needed to be joined with her completely. I needed to find my pleasure with hers.

"Tessa," I bit out.

She drew back, releasing me with a soft pop. "I need you," I nearly growled.

It was a tumble and a fumble as we

yanked at each other across the short distance from the door to her bed. We left a trail of clothes behind us. I crawled onto the bed and pulled her on top of me, savoring her silky soft skin, her warmth, and the lush give of her curves.

With one arm around her waist, I pressed a palm into the mattress, levering myself up and back until I was partially seated against the pillows. "Right here, sweetheart," I murmured.

Straddling me, she shimmied up and over me. I gripped her on one hip and palmed her cheek with my other hand. I surged up just as she sank down, sheathing me in her slick channel.

She let out something between a sigh and a whimper. I nudged a little deeper. "Look at me, sweetheart."

Her lashes lifted, and I was ensnared in her dark gaze. There was a fusion of desire, fierce, raw lust, and a deep, abiding love that spun through all of this moment. It cinched the threads holding us together tighter and tighter.

"I love you," I murmured against her mouth in a lazy, open kiss.

The moment was slow and sensual as I rocked into her, feeling the brush of her nipples on my chest and savoring the way she began to tremble. I knew her body. I knew just what she needed. I waited until I felt her shudder deeply and go completely still for a millisecond before she cried out. I captured her cry with a kiss, and my own release sizzled like burning lightning.

Chapter Thirty-Seven

TESSA

Adam held me close as my climax rolled through me in deep, rippling waves, the pleasure bone-deep. It went far beyond pure physical release with the emotional intensity feeding into the fire of my release until I collapsed against him.

His fingers tightened in my hair when I felt him rock into me one last time, and the heat of his release filled me as he shuddered and jerked against me. I didn't know how long we stayed like that—joined and wrapped together. I just wanted to breathe with him, to feel completely at one with him.

Eventually, I lifted my head. He was right there, waiting for me, brushing my tangled hair away from my cheeks and kissing me.

Because it was this kind of love, when my stomach growled, his lips curled in a slow smile. "When's the last time you ate?"

"I don't even know."

After we disentangled ourselves, Adam ordered pizza, and we ate it on my bed with the box between us. Eric must've been exhausted because he didn't even wake up when the delivery person rang the doorbell.

I fell asleep, warm and safe, in Adam's embrace. For the first time in years, I wasn't worried about what might happen the next day. The details would work themselves out.

Chapter Thirty-Eight

TESSA

"Well?" McKenna pressed, her eyes twinkling with a sly gleam.

"Well, what?" I countered.

My friend rolled her eyes and nudged me with her elbow before she shifted her gaze to Adam who stood on my other side holding my hand.

"Can you just admit it? Are you engaged? What's the plan?" she asked.

A laugh sputtered out. "What do you mean?"

McKenna let out a little sigh. "I admitted it when I broke our pact."

"Pact?" Adam prompted.

"Tessa and I had a pact." Out of reflex, we bumped fists quickly. "Neither one of us was ever going to have a relationship. And then, I met Jack." McKenna's cheeks went a little pink as Jack strolled up behind her, slipped his arms around her waist, and dusted a kiss on the side of her neck.

"Ohhhhh," Adam said slowly. I felt my own cheeks heating when I met his eyes. "It completely makes sense."

Although his eyes twinkled, I could feel the sincerity threaded within the laughter. It *did* make sense for me at the time.

I glanced back at McKenna. "I broke the pact, but I have no idea when we're getting engaged or anything like that."

McKenna let out an impatient sigh. "I would love to plan another wedding."

"You got a black eye at the last wedding you planned," Blake said as he approached our group.

McKenna giggled. "It was totally an accident and all Jack's fault."

Jack chuckled. A woman waiting in line nearby looked askance at Jack. "I did open a door into McKenna's face, but it was truly an accident."

Adam reached over, tugging lightly on the end of McKenna's ponytail as he commented, "When the time is right, we'll let you know."

I smiled up at him just as Rhys and

Haven came walking in. We hadn't planned to meet this way, but Spill the Beans Café was the heartbeat of Fireweed Harbor, so it wasn't a surprise that we all ended up here on a chilly autumn morning.

"Where is—" Blake began just as Kenan and Quinn walked in with Wyatt and Griffin behind them.

I glanced among the Cannon siblings, rolling my eyes slightly. "There's no shortage of you all," I quipped.

As if on cue, Fiona and Rosie came walking in. Rosie was clearly on the way to work, wearing a pair of hot-pink nursing scrubs while Fiona had her apron on.

Blake glanced over and burst out laughing. "Babe, you forgot to take your apron off. You better be careful, or —"

Phyllis cut in from behind the counter. "We could use you for some help with the baking."

Fiona smiled as she untied her apron. "I went in early this morning. We have an event tonight, but I wanted to get things prepped to be baked later. For what it's worth, I'm going back as soon as I get some coffee."

My heart felt warm. I was still marveling at the sense of relief and peace I felt. Rich was awaiting his trial in jail. Despite his father's attempt to get him out on bail, the court had denied it. I couldn't help but experience a little flare of satisfaction when I was present in court when the judge refused to grant bail due to the severity of his charges. Rich's charges were even more severe since he committed them with a firearm.

Colin had filed for me to have full custody without any visitation rights the day after the whole fiasco. He'd already sent over a proposal to Rich's attorney for him to relinquish his rights. Colin had assured me that if I felt like Rich was safe in the future, I could support visits with Eric, but this would prevent him from being able to take me back to court again and again as he'd been doing.

In a surprise, at least for me, Barb had left Rich's father. We'd had a few tentative lunches together. While she loved her son dearly, his actions had shocked and frightened her. Even though she had yet to be open about it, I suspected the trauma she experienced being with her husband for so long would take her some time to get over. She was very reticent to speak of it, but she seemed genuinely remorseful for not supporting me when I left before.

Adam squeezed my hip lightly where his palm rested on it. I glanced up. All it took was a subtle touch from him, and I went all gooey inside. Sweet hell. I loved this man, and there'd been a time I didn't even think love was a possibility.

"Tessa?" he prompted in his clear, low voice.

"What?"

"Do you want to sit down?" A slight smile teased at the corners of his mouth.

I got that warm and tingly feeling in my belly. That feeling was specifically connected to Adam.

"Yes, please," I finally said.

Rosie had stopped beside us, and she glanced from me to Adam and back again. "If I didn't know better, I might think you were tipsy. You look loopy."

"She's in lo-o-o-ve," Haven teased.

I smiled among my friends, feeling happier than I could've imagined. It was hard to consider I'd be this happy simply getting coffee. I recalled the way I used to feel back when I was still married to Rich. I was constantly alert and anxious when I was out in public, always worried somebody might notice something was wrong. Even when I was alone, I'd kept my guard up.

Now, I just wanted to hug all my friends and shout out my joy to the universe. Which, given the recent events, maybe seemed too much, but traumatic events tended to bring things into sharp focus.

On the heels of a shaky breath, I smiled back at Rosie. "I'm not tipsy, but I just feel good."

My friend's gaze sobered. "You deserve it."

Adam's palm shifted to the center of my lower back, coaxing me toward a table. Over the next hour or so, we chatted and had coffee. It was one of the best mornings I'd ever had.

Chapter Thirty-Nine

ADAM

Six months later

I held up the baseball glove. "One more!" I called to Eric, who stood across from me in our backyard.

He lifted his arm and threw the ball with all of his might, socking it straight to me. I caught it. "Good throw!"

Eric had settled in well. There was no doubt he carried some anxiety and trauma from what had happened with his dad. It wasn't specifically that last night because he hadn't known what was really happening until the last few minutes. But the first five years of his life had been spent with the overbearing and abusive presence of his father, and that had shaped him. He wanted approval from adults fiercely. He was almost too well-behaved.

I approached him and saw that flicker of hesitation and worry in his gaze. "You throw better than me."

A smile cracked across his face when I reached out to ruffle his hair before giving him a light squeeze on one of his shoulders.

"I think we're cooking tonight," I said as we began walking toward the back porch, which had a door that led into the kitchen.

"Mom is doing the weather report tonight?" He was rubbing his fingers together with one hand, a nervous habit I'd noticed. I wanted to erase all of his anxiety, but I knew from my own experience it would take time, and there would always be triggers to manage.

"Yep, she is. We'll watch it while we get dinner ready."

He looked up at me. "Do we have to cook?"

"Pizza?" I teased.

"Can we?"

"Deal. We cook most nights when your mom's working," I pointed out as I held the door open for him.

He skipped ahead of me before spinning back as he set the baseball in a little cubby by the door, taking the glove from me when I handed it over.

"I know we do. Mom loves that about you," he replied with a smile.

My heart gave a rounding kick. I was so gone for Tessa that any positive feedback about how she felt about me made my heart happy.

"I hope so. I love watching her do the weather report."

Eric stopped, peering up at me. His gaze sobered. "You really do." He blinked. "You're not like my dad. At all. You don't even get mad."

This time, my heart gave an achy beat. "There's not much to get mad about." I knelt to meet him at eye level. "Here's something important to understand. Everybody gets mad. You say I don't get mad much, but it's all about how you handle it."

Eric studied me. "You don't yell or say mean things."

"Remember when you and your mom came to my office last week?" Eric nodded quickly. "I was actually kind of mad at my brother."

"Which one?"

I chuckled at that. "It could've been any of them. In this case, it was Kenan."

"But he's your twin brother."

"True, and I love him very much like all my siblings, but I was mad, or maybe annoyed, because he forgot something, and I had to go out of my way to deal with it. Right before you showed up, I had just told him not to waste my time again."

"That was it?"

"That was it. You don't know what my life was like when I was a little boy, but my grandfather used to lose his temper a lot, just like your dad. He's in jail too. Everybody gets mad. You'll get mad sometimes too, but it'll be okay."

He studied me, his brow wrinkling in concentration before he nodded slowly. "Okay."

We ordered pepperoni pizza because it was his favorite and mine. Rich was safely in prison for many years and had agreed to relinquish his parental rights. It didn't even seem that he cared to try to have a relationship with Eric, which infuriated me because it was so clear he'd only maintained that connection to hurt Tessa. I was beyond relieved that Tessa and Eric were safe and that the legal process had concluded.

Once settled in the living room with our

pizza, Eric and I watched the news and weather report. I loved that even though our evenings weren't always with Tessa, I got to see her anyway.

A few hours later, Eric went to bed, and she came out to the kitchen where I was tidying up. She smiled at me. "Pizza night, huh? You deserve it. You've been cooking every night. Thanks for waiting for me and saving some."

"I'll always wait for you," I murmured just before I bent to kiss her.

EPILOGUE

Wyatt Cannon

As I jogged to the elevator, I saw a flash of auburn hair ahead. My hand caught the doors just before they closed, and I stepped in quickly. I knew that hair.

"Rosie?"

Rosie Alder was looking down at her phone. Her head whipped up. "Wyatt? What are you doing here?"

"Probably the same thing as you. I'm here for a family vacation. Does McKenna know you're here?" I asked, referring to my sister who happened to be Rosie's close friend.

Rosie's mossy-green eyes studied me before she nodded. I hadn't even tapped the floor number, but I glanced over to see the elevator was, logically, stopping on the floor to the main lobby.

As we stepped out together, I added, "Vegas is certainly a change of pace from Fireweed Harbor."

Rosie's laughter was soft. When I glanced down at her, she was looking across the lobby. In addition to being one of my sister's best friends, she was close with the various sisters-in-law who had joined my family in the past few years.

Rosie and I had been doing a little dance around each other. I'd had a thing for her for years, yet she kept me and every guy at arm's length. Then we'd had a week that was seared into my memory. She had been in Fireweed Harbor for a week after graduating from college and before leaving for nursing school. I had to force those memories away often. The one time I'd said anything to her about it, she'd told me to forget it ever happened.

"Where are you headed?" I asked.

Rosie stopped, looking up at me. When I glanced down, my eyes dipped even further. She wore a fitted silky blouse that flared around the sweet curves of her hips. Rosie had the hot tomboy vibe going strong. She was independent, opinionated, and impossible for me to forget.

It had been easier before I'd moved back to Fireweed Harbor a year ago. Now, our social circles collided all the time. Our shared hometown was small, and we had almost all of our friends in common.

"I was going —"

Rosie was cut off when my sister's voice rang out. "Rosie!"

"Wyatt," McKenna added as she hurried over to us through the crowd. "Oh my gosh, I'm so glad you're here!" my sister exclaimed when she stopped beside us.

I glanced over at my sister. "You knew I was here. We're all here," I pointed out.

McKenna had insisted we needed to go on a vacation together, and she got some package deal for a trip to Vegas for the family and some friends.

"I know, but I didn't know Rosie had made it yet, and Tessa and Adam are getting married! They're eloping! We can go to the wedding," McKenna explained.

"Married?" Rosie's tone was decidedly skeptical.

McKenna nodded, her smile wide. "Wyatt can be your date."

Rosie's cheeks went a little pink, and I wanted to kiss her. Hell, every time I saw her, I remembered what it was like to kiss her. I liked to have fun as much as any guy, but what I'd had with Rosie during our brief fling had been beyond memorable. I'd been too young to genuinely appreciate it. Now that I was older, wiser, and even a little bitter, I knew what we'd had was good.

None of us were surprised Adam and Tessa were actually getting married. The only surprise was the details.

Later, as we were having dinner at a nearby casino, I made a toast with a quick smile around the table. "To the amazing couple and to weddings in Vegas. They're efficient and easy."

When I glanced over, I noticed Adam looking down at Tessa. The bitterness and cold that encased my heart thawed a little. Adam had always been one to love easily. The only two left unmarried in our sibling group at this point were my twin brother, Griffin, and me.

If I ever got married, it might as well be Vegas. I wasn't much for pomp and circumstance. Hours later, we had all thrown ourselves into the Vegas vibe with lots of laughs and even a little gambling. I won a good round, so I was feeling more joyful than usual.

Even Rosie loosened up, although she and

I had only enjoyed one round of drinks. She was laughing at something Blake said as he got up to leave the table. He had his hand firmly curled around Fiona's. "All right, you two are the last ones standing. Make it good." He tapped his knuckles on the table before he strolled away with Fiona. He slipped his arm around his wife's waist, pulling her close as they walked.

I pondered our now almost empty table, save Rosie and me. She sat directly across from me. I was sure that had to be pure chance. "So," she began. "Who will it be next?"

"What do you mean?"

"You or Griffin? You're the last two Cannon siblings who aren't married."

I studied her, feeling a little reckless and restless to act on the desire that had never stopped simmering since our fling.

I shrugged. "I don't know. What do you say we send this night out with a bang?"

She eyed me for a long moment before standing. "Let's."

———

The following morning, I woke slowly, cataloging a pounding headache and a warm, silky soft body curled beside me. My hand was curled over the lush curve of Rosie's bottom.

I didn't remember much, but I did remember a wild kiss in the elevator and then tumbling through the door into this room. There were other flashes of memory. I didn't want to wake Rosie up. I wanted her to stay exactly where she was.

Maybe I didn't remember all the details, but I knew last night had been amazing.

I rolled my bad shoulder slightly. I'd injured it a few too many times while firefighting. As I moved, I became aware of a sensation on my hand. I dragged my eyes open and lifted my left hand to see a wedding ring on my ring finger.

What the actual fuck?

Rosie shifted beside me just as I started to panic. Her eyes blinked open, and she raised her head. We stared at each other for a few beats before she shifted again and lifted her left hand. She also wore a wedding ring.

"Oh. I remember coming into your room and—"

"Oh is one way to put it."

Her cheeks flushed a deep shade of pink. "What happened after that?"

.   .   .

Thank you for reading Adam & Tessa's story! Want a glimpse of the future for them? Join my newsletter to receive an exclusive scene.

Sign up here: https://BookHip.com/PFH MQHK

p.s. If you are already subscribed, you'll still be able to access the scene.

Up next in the Fireweed Harbor Series is Ever After All!

Rosie & Wyatt are living a cliche. They got married in Vegas after a hot night together.

Rosie wishes her impulsive marriage was a joke. She's convinced it's a huge mistake and plans to file for divorce ASAP, preferably yesterday.

Meanwhile, Wyatt wants a real chance with Rosie. He thinks they could have it all. Wyatt takes *he-falls-first* to the next level as he fights to prove that what they have is worth it all.

Don't miss Wyatt & Rosie's intense, swoony romance that starts with marriage and ends with HEA!

One-click: Ever After All - available August 2023!

For more swoony romance...

This Crazy Love kicks off the Swoon Series - small town southern romance with enough heat to melt you! Jackson & Shay's story is epic - swoon-worthy & intensely emotional. Jackson just happens to be Shay's brother's best friend. He's also *seriously* easy on the eyes. Shay has a past, the kind of past she would most definitely like to forget. Past or not, Jackson is about to rock her world. Don't miss their story!

Burn For Me is a second chance romance for the ages. Sexy firefighters? Check. Rugged men? Check. Wrapped up together? Check. Brave the fire in this hot, small-town romance. Amelia & Cade were high school sweethearts & then it all fell apart. When they cross paths again, it's epic - don't miss Cade's story!

For more small town romance, take a visit to Last Frontier Lodge in Diamond Creek. A sexy, alpha SEAL meets his match with a brainy heroine in Take Me Home. Marley is all brains & Gage is all brawn. Sparks fly when their worlds collide. Don't miss Gage & Marley's story!

If sports romance lights your spark, check out The Play. Liam is a British footballer who falls for Olivia, his doctor. A twist of forbidden heats up this swoon-worthy & laugh-out-loud romance. Don't miss Liam & Olivia's story.

ACKNOWLEDGMENTS

If you made it all the way to this page, thank you, thank you, thank you. I am so very grateful for my readers. Writing can be lonely and every story feels like making a wish and wondering if anyone will hear it. Thank you for reading and for giving my stories a chance.

I'm deeply thankful to my editor who patiently does her best to help me make my stories better. Many thanks to my proofreader who must sigh when I lose count of days in a story by this point, so please know any remaining mistakes are mine alone.

Najla Qamber created another gorgeous cover. My assistant helps me look like I might have it together. I honestly don't know how I'd do this author life without her patience and kindness. Hugs to my PR guru, Dani Sanchez at Wildfire Marketing, for holding my hand while I navigate the treach-

erous waters of actually talking about my
books, to anyone, anywhere.

To my family, my friends and my dogs, who are family and love me just because.

xoxo

J.H. Croix

5) Follow me on Instagram at <u>https://www.</u>
<u>instagram.com/jhcroix/</u>
6) Like my Facebook page at <u>https://www.</u>
<u>facebook.com/jhcroix</u>

———

Fireweed Harbor Series
Make You Mine
Dare To Fall
Be The One
One More Time
Wait For You
Ever After All - due out August 2024!
Light My Fire Series
Wild With You
Hold Me Now
Only Ever Us
Fall For Me
Keep Me Close
With Every Breath
All It Takes
Take Me Now
Meant To Be
Dare With Me Series
Crash Into You
Evers & Afters
Come To Me
Back To Us

Take Me There
After We Fall
Swoon Series
This Crazy Love
Wait For Me
Break My Fall
Truly Madly Mine
Still Go Crazy
If We Dare
Steal My Heart
Into The Fire Series
Burn For Me
Slow Burn
Burn So Bad
Hot Mess
Burn So Good
Sweet Fire
Play With Fire
Melt With You
Burn For You
Crash & Burn
That Snowy Night
Brit Boys Sports Romance
The Play
Big Win
Out Of Bounds
Play Me
Naughty Wish
Diamond Creek Alaska Novels

When Love Comes
Follow Love
Love Unbroken
Love Untamed
Tumble Into Love
Christmas Nights

Lodge Series
Take Me Home
Love at Last
Just This Once
Falling Fast
Stay With Me
When We Fall
Hold Me Close
Crazy For You
Just Us

ABOUT THE AUTHOR

USA Today Bestselling Author J. H. Croix lives in a small town with her husband and two spoiled dogs. Croix writes contemporary romance with sassy women and alpha men who aren't afraid to show some emotion. Her love for quirky small-towns and the characters that inhabit them shines through in her writing. Take a walk on the wild side of romance with her bestselling novels!

Places you can find me:
jhcroixauthor.com
jhcroix@jhcroix.com

facebook.com/jhcroix

instagram.com/jhcroix

bookbub.com/authors/j-h-croix